The concert left Joe tense and exhausted

Quincy checked to see if he was awake, and found him watching her with half-raised lids. He lazily put out a hand and pulled her down toward him. She let herself curl against his body, her mouth dry as Joe tipped up her chin and began to kiss her softly.

She did not feel she was in any danger; he was far too tired.

Her lips parted beneath his. He murmured something, his hand at her waist, and slid sideways, drawing her with him so that they lay on the couch entwined. Her body jerked with shock as Joe's fingers moved inside her robe.

"No," she gasped. She put a hand up to thrust him away, but he caught it.

"I need you," he breathed huskily.

CHARLOTTE LAMB
is also the author of these

Harlequin Presents

and these
Harlequin Romances

Many of these titles are available at your local bookseller.

For a free catalog listing all titles currently available,
send your name and address to:

HARLEQUIN READER SERVICE
1440 South Priest Drive, Tempe, AZ 85281
Canadian address: Stratford, Ontario N5A 6W2

CHARLOTTE LAMB

a wild affair

Harlequin Books

TORONTO • NEW YORK • LOS ANGELES • LONDON
AMSTERDAM • PARIS • SYDNEY • HAMBURG
STOCKHOLM • ATHENS • TOKYO • MILAN

Harlequin Presents first edition November 1982
ISBN 0-373-10545-2

Original hardcover edition published in 1982
by Mills & Boon Limited

CHAPTER ONE

Quincy was just about to start making supper; her mind divided between macaroni cheese and Brendan's blow-by-blow account of how he had delivered a calf a few hours earlier. A tall, thin young man with dusty blond hair, he had only been practising as a vet for five years and was still at the stage of thinking his job the most enthralling subject in the world, and Quincy, being the daughter of Brendan's partner and therefore accustomed to talk of the medical problems of the animal world, seemed to him the perfect audience. She was not merely a pretty girl, but one likely to listen and applaud Brendan's great triumph. It had been a difficult birth, touch and go for a while, but Brendan Leary had won against all the odds and he wanted someone to appreciate it. The farmer had clapped him on the shoulder and given him a stiff whisky afterwards, he might even pay his bill eventually, but Brendan needed more than that.

Quincy listened, smiling, and although she wasn't saying anything she was looking every bit as impressed as Brendan could hope—she had been listening to such stories all her life, she was fond of Brendan and she was always happy to hear of his triumphs in the face of the thousand and one disasters which could befall his patients.

Her parents were having dinner out that evening, to celebrate Mrs Jones's birthday. Quincy could hear her mother singing in the bath while Mr Jones shaved, his electric razor buzzing. in counterpoint to his wife's faintly unsteady contralto. From Bobby's bedroom came the transatlantic babble of his radio—Quincy's brother claimed to be unable to do his homework unless his ears were safely plugged with pop music, a theory his father disputed but had given up trying to argue over with Bobby.

It was a warm spring evening and Quincy had no sense of foreboding, no warning premonition, as she unearthed the cheese grater and filled a saucepan with water in which to boil the macaroni.

When the doorbell went Brendan stopped talking and groaned: 'I knew I'd be called out again! Why is there always an emergency when I'm on call?'

Quincy laughed, shedding her apron. 'Don't be so pessimistic, it's probably Penny, she said she might drive over for a chat.' As she left the kitchen Brendan stared after her gloomily, convinced of the worst. He had used up most of his energy during the day and had been looking forward to a quiet evening with Quincy. She had invited him to supper, as he was on call, and the last thing he wanted to do was spend hours in a draughty cowshed instead of talking to Quincy. She was so easy to talk to—slim, green-eyed, smiling, with short chestnut hair which sprang in soft curls around her face, she had a feminine warmth Brendan found very appealing.

Quincy walked down the hall and opened the front door, then froze in disbelief as she stared at the man outside. She was so amazed as she recognised him that she didn't notice the people jostling behind his wide shoulders. She just stared at that unmistakable face, open-mouthed.

'Hallo, Quincy,' he said in a deep, warm voice, smil-

ing, and then all hell was let loose around her: flash-
bulbs exploded in her face, men jostled around them,
voices yelled questions she hardly heard, the constant
explosions of light dazzled and blinded her.

'How does it feel to have a dream come true,
Quincy?'

'Look this way, sweetie, smile . . .'

'Did you ever think you'd win, Quincy?'

Quincy's mind was blown to smithereens—this
wasn't happening, she was having some sort of brain-
storm, it couldn't be real. Who were all these people,
and what on earth were they talking about? She blinked
as one of them darted at her, aiming his camera so
close she saw stars for a few seconds. When she opened
her eyes again she hoped they would all have gone,
vanished back into the warm spring night from which
they had sprung, but when she opened her eyes they
were all still there, snapping around her like hungry
barracuda, bawling questions she didn't understand
and could not answer, grabbing her arm on first this
side and then that, whirling her like a dervish.

It seemed at the time to last for an eternity, but later
she realised it had happened with such speed that it
could only have been a couple of minutes from the
second when she opened that door, blithely unaware
of what was about to hit her, until the instant when
Joe Aldonez took a step forward, and, as she quickly
looked at him in unnerved query, smiled reassuringly
at her.

'Don't look so alarmed,' he murmured.

'Can we have a kiss, Mr Aldonez?' one of the photographers yelled, and the others took up the cry. 'Hey,
Joe, kiss her, would you?'

The next minute Quincy felt the world swing wildly

as she was caught into Joe Aldonez's arms. Her short
chestnut curls spilled over his sleeve as he tilted her,
face upward. Afraid she was going to fall, she grabbed
at his shoulders and then his hard, warm mouth
engulfed her lips. Quincy had her eyes open for the
first few seconds, until the constant explosion of flash-
lights forced her to close them.

I'm going out of my mind, she thought. I'm having
delusions, this is a hallucination—it can't be happening.

If it was a hallucination, it was strangely potent. Her
lips trembled under the sensual movements of his
mouth, her body quivering as a gentle hand pressed
along her spine, but Quincy had a solid core of
common sense. She kept her eyes shut and told herself
firmly that it wasn't real. What was happening was
happening inside her own head, she was dreaming on
her feet, and in a minute she would open her eyes,
looking very silly, to find herself staring at the irate
and puzzled owner of a sick cow.

'What on earth——?'

Good question, Quincy thought, still clinging helplessly to the man holding her and half believing she
was imagining that voice, too, until it bellowed like an
angry bull.

'What's going on, for heaven's sake?'

The next minute she was free, glassy-eyed and very
flushed, shaking like a leaf while she stared at her father
in his old woolly check dressing-gown, standing at the
top of the stairs and gaping down at her and the all-
too-real circus which was continuing to perform noisily
around her.

The photographers took pictures of him, too, and
Quincy saw her mother scuttling behind Mr Jones,

clutching at the lapels of her blue quilted dressing-gown, as she stared, wide-eyed, at the invasion of her home.

'Well, isn't anyone going to answer me?' Robert Jones demanded.

Everyone tried to answer him at once, the confused gabble merely making him scowl, then Joe Aldonez moved, so fast that Quincy for one wasn't aware what he was doing until it was done, his strategy carried through so smoothly that it met no opposition.

'Thank you, gentlemen, we'll wrap it up for the evening. I'm sure you've got enough pictures now, and Carmen will keep you informed,' he said briskly, driving the press before him like sheep. No doubt they would have resisted had he not appeared to be going with them, his long stride pushing them all backwards, mesmerised by his confidence. The minute they were all outside, the door closed. Angry shouts of 'Hey!' and the thud of fists on the door made it clear that the press were annoyed, but that did not seem to worry Joe Aldonez.

'They'll go in a minute or two,' he told Mr Jones coolly. 'They've got what they came for.' What was that? Quincy wondered, still trying to convince herself that she was not the victim of an hallucination.

Joe Aldonez was not the only person left behind by the tide of press men—with him was a man in a pale blue suit who had said nothing but who kept on smiling, and a blonde girl in a fur-lined sheepskin coat which she wore with an air of elegance Quincy couldn't quite define. Nothing the girl was wearing seemed particularly striking—it was just the way she wore it which left that impression of chic.

'Sorry about the rumpus,' the blonde girl was saying

to Mr Jones with a friendly smile which didn't quite
ring true—it had a certain careful deliberation which
Quincy didn't like. 'I'm afraid it got out of hand there
for a minute or two. We should have rung to warn you
we were coming, but we wanted to give Quincy a real
surprise.'

They had certainly done that. Quincy was beginning
to recover from the traumatic shock which the light-
ning-speed sequence of events had kept her locked in
ever since she opened that door, and now she was getting annoyed.

'What . . .' she began, and the blonde girl turned
towards her, holding out her hand. 'Congratulations,
Quincy,' she said, the trace of amused patronage in her
face and voice making the hair on the back of Quincy's
neck prickle angrily.

'What are you talking about? And who are you?'
Quincy hadn't looked at Joe Aldonez since the door
shut, but she was constantly aware of him, although
she couldn't yet allow herself to believe he was really
there in person. Had he actually erupted into her life,
or was she having some sort of Alice-in-Wonderland
dream? Would she wake up in a minute and realise
none of this had happened?

'You've won,' the blonde girl said.

'What are you talking about?' Quincy asked.

That was the question which was bothering her
father, too. He came down the stairs now, bristling
like a porcupine, his damp hair standing up in spikes,
and asked it very insistently: 'What's this all about?'

Smiling, the blonde girl offered him her hand and
he slowly accepted it without thinking, staring at her.

'Who are you?'

'I'm Carmen Lister, the editor of *Vibes*. You must

be Quincy's father—hallo, Mr Jones.'

'What on earth is *Vibes*?' Mr Jones asked in a harassed voice, rumpling his hair with one hand, and the blonde girl laughed.

'A music magazine.'

'Are you a friend of my daughter?' Mr Jones asked in bemused uncertainty. 'What were all those photographers doing here? Why were they taking pictures of my daughter?' His eyes moved round to Joe Aldonez, his frown came back. 'And who's that man who was kissing her?'

A genuine expression flitted over Carmen Lister's carefully smiling face—Quincy pinned it down as a mixture of incredulity and shock.

'That's Joe Aldonez, Mr Jones,' Carmen told him, throwing a look of apology in the direction of the other man.

'Who?' Mr Jones said and Carmen almost winced.

'Joe's a big *star*,' she said.

Mrs Jones had found her way downstairs by now and was staring open-mouthed at Joe Aldonez, her expression making it clear that she, at least, knew who he was—but then so did most women. His records had been hitting the top ten regularly ever since his first disc came out; his deep, husky voice sending shivers down the back of any woman listening as he smokily whispered out love songs which had a smouldering sexiness.

'*Vibes* has been running a competition,' Carmen explained. 'You had to answer six questions about Joe's songs and decide which pair of eyes belonged to him— we had a dozen pairs to choose from, it's surprising how difficult that is, I had a job deciding which was the right pair myself.' She smiled and Mr Jones gazed blankly at her. 'The first prize was a date with Joe,' Carmen told him. 'And your daughter won.'

'I can't have!' Quincy broke out involuntarily.

Carmen turned and gave her a smile as genuine as the disbelief with which she had realised that Mr Jones hadn't recognised Joe Aldonez.

'You have, I promise you,' she said. 'You must be thrilled.'

'I can't have won,' Quincy insisted, and Carmen laughed.

'I assure you, you have.' She had rather sharp blue eyes, their lids heavily painted with silvery blue eyeshadow, and her lashes were visibly false; clustering in dramatic sweeps which flicked up and down every time she opened and closed her eyes. They gave her the appearance of a doll, her blonde hair neatly curled around her face, but the faint hardness of her expression when she wasn't smiling so carefully contradicted that pretty, doll-like look.

'Quincy entered this competition and won?' Mr Jones demanded, staring at his daughter as though he had never seen her before, disgust in his face. Mr Jones did not like pop music—his own taste inclined towards brass bands playing martial tunes—and he was appalled by the thought of Quincy entering a competition with a date with a pop star as the first prize.

A man of fifty, Robert Jones was wiry and active; his skin freshly coloured from years of working in the open air in all weathers, his eyes brown, his hair almost the same colour although it was slowly gathering streaks of grey which he resented and tried to brush out of sight. He was a man of common sense and quiet humour; his veterinary practice was very busy, but his love of animals helped him to accept the heavy work load his job enforced. He was popular with both his patients and their owners, because his temper was even, his patience almost inexhaustible and his manner cheerful. His one vice was his pipe, which he smoked in secret with an air of guilty satisfaction and constantly resolved to give up.

'Quincy's a very lucky girl,' Carmen told him. 'We had thousands of entries—even I was surprised by the flood of mail we got, we had to take on extra staff to cope with it all.'

'Good heavens,' Mr Jones muttered, still staring at Quincy. 'Quincy, I can't understand why you did such a thing!'

'But I didn't,' she protested, her voice almost shrill in her determination to be heard.

Joe Aldonez moved and her eyes flew round to meet his stare. 'You didn't what?' he asked slowly. His speaking voice had the same husky, smoky quality which had made his singing so immediately recognisable, and it sent exactly the same shiver down her spine. His American accent was soft and drawling, far more noticeable than when he sang.

'Enter,' she explained, studying his face and struck by the odd contradictions in it—the harsh power of the bone structure giving an angularity to cheek and jaw, to the deep forehead and long arrogant nose, which was offset by a startling beauty in the deep, dark wells of his eyes. The same clash was revealed in his mouth; the upper lip firm and cool, the lower warm and distinctly sensual, curving in a half-smile as she stared at him, which made her flush.

His brows winged upwards in a sardonic movement. 'You didn't enter the competition?'

'I didn't,' she insisted.

Carmen's brows met. 'What do you mean? I have your entry form here with me!' She unzipped her shoulder bag and produced a crumpled page, torn from the magazine judging by the look of it, and waved it at Quincy. 'See? You are Quincy Jones, aren't you?'

'Yes,' Quincy admitted. 'But . . .'

'And this is your address?' Carmen's voice had an irritated ring.

Quincy took the form from her, and looked at it. Her own name leapt up at her, printed in capital letters, below it her address printed in the same hand. 'I don't understand it,' she said, her face puzzled.

'We haven't got time for games,' Carmen dismissed with a shrug. 'I'm sure your parents won't object, if that's what's worrying you, there's no need to pretend you didn't enter.'

'I'm not pretending anything,' said Quincy, then her eye fell on the handwriting lower down on the form and she gave a choked cry of recognition. As she looked up she saw her brother lurking on the top of the stairs, and yelled: 'Bobby!'

He at once began to vanish, but her father had been looking over her shoulder at the form and he, too, had recognised the handwriting.

'Bobby, you come down here!' he shouted, and Bobby stopped in his tracks. Wearing a silly smile he came down, a step at a time, while everyone stared at him. His face had gone brick-red, a colour which shrieked at his mop of untidy ginger hair and the gaudy yellow T-shirt he was wearing. As he got to the hall, his father's heavy hand descended on his shoulder and Bobby looked up at him, his expression placatory.

'Did you fill in that entry form?' Robert Jones demanded.

Bobby didn't utter a syllable, he just nodded. Even the tips of his large ears were crimson—although Bobby's hair was pretty unusual, it was his ears which most people remembered and which were responsible for his school nickname, Jugs, or, when his friends weren't in a hurry, Jughandle. Bobby was fifteen and lived in a state of happy squalor, his room cluttered with the assorted debris of a very busy life: model planes standing on every surface or suspended from the ceiling, clothes left wherever he happened to drop them, books and magazines in untidy piles all over the room. Mrs Jones had a blitz on the room once a week, but no sooner had Bobby been allowed back into it again than he set about restoring it to its usual condition. 'Anyone would think that boy had been born in a dustbin!' Mr Jones often complained.

'Why did you put your sister's name down?' Joe Aldonez asked, and Bobby shot him a wary look. 'Why not your own?' Joe asked.

'Well, it was for girls, wasn't it?' Bobby mumbled.

'Then why did you enter?' Carmen asked furiously, and Mr Jones nodded in agreement. 'Yes, why did you enter?' he chimed.

Bobby became speechless again, shuffling his feet. Joe Aldonez was watching him thoughtfully, one long index finger scratching the side of his jaw as he considered the subject. 'I get it,' he said suddenly. 'You wanted to win one of the transistors, right?'

'Right,' said Bobby, brightening up.

'What?' Mr Jones demanded.

'There were transistor radios as runner-up prizes,' Joe explained. 'Fifty of them, good ones, too.'

'Bobby Jones, I could kill you!' Quincy snapped, erupting into fury.

'That wouldn't solve anything,' Joe Aldonez told her with amusement.

'It would make me feel a lot happier,' retorted Quincy, keeping her eyes on her brother as he edged away.

Carmen Lister had gone red, too, but not with embarrassment, with sheer, blinding rage; her blue eyes glittering like the Northern Lights, very bright and cold. 'You mean, we've driven all this way from London, set up all that publicity, released the story and gone to all this trouble, and now we've got to start all over again with some other girl?' She wasn't so much talking to any of them as to herself, her voice raw with fury, and Quincy could imagine that she was not exactly an easy lady to work with, especially if you had made a little mistake.

Everyone looked at her. Mr Jones tightened his grip on his son's shoulder. Mrs Jones looked worried and Quincy took a step backward as if afraid Carmen Lister might turn dangerous at any minte, only to tread on Brendan's toe and glance round in startled surprise at his stifled yelp. 'Sorry,' she whispered, rather relieved to find him there.

'What are we going to do?' Carmen was saying, looking at the man in the perfectly tailored blue suit who had not spoken a word yet but had been listening attentively and watching them all. He had a face which was far from easy to read; it had a smooth, plastic look, the smile it wore as prefabricated as the one Carmen usually wore, switching on and off like a faulty light bulb. His eyes were knife-sharp; his pale hair, closely shaven face and well-groomed clothes seemed to help him merge into whatever background he was placed against, but gave away nothing about his real personality—as if, whatever he was, he preferred not to be seen being it in public. He looked, thought Quincy, like a perfectly cloned politician.

'I'm sure we can sort out this little hitch,' he said. His voice was American, Quincy noted. Smiling, he held out his hand to Robert Jones. 'I'm Billy Griffith, Joe's manager, Mr Jones.'

'How do you do?' Mr Jones said stiffly, shaking hands.

'Glad to know you,' said Billy Griffith. 'Now, why don't we have a little chat about this, man to man?' He took hold of Robert Jones's elbow and steered him through the open door of the sitting-room before Mr Jones had had time to work out what was happening. Mrs Jones and Carmen Lister followed, but as Quincy moved she found herself facing a closed door. Flushing, she was about to push it open again when Joe Aldonez stepped into her path and smiled down at her.

'You know, I think we could all do with some coffee.'

'I want to know what they're saying in there,' Quincy said crossly. She was certain Carmen Lister had deliberately shut the door on her. A conspiracy was being hatched behind that door and Quincy wanted no part of it.

The phone began to shrill and Brendan said: 'I'll take that in the surgery.' He walked towards the interconnecting door which led from the house into the one-storey building which had been built on to the side of the house to act as a surgery, and switched the call through as he passed the phone. Bobby was staring at Joe Aldonez, whose dark eyes had followed Brendan briefly.

'You look just like your pictures,' he accused.

'Is that a compliment or a complaint?' Joe enquired, turning his black head to look down at him, his mouth curving into an amused smile. He must be well over six foot, Quincy realised, measuring him against her five-foot-five brother. Against that night-black hair, his skin was smooth and bronzed, betraying the fact that he came from a much warmer climate than the West of England.

'I suppose I don't get a transistor now?' Bobby asked gloomily.

'In your place I'd let the subject drop,' Joe drawled with dry amusement.

'I did win!' Bobby protested, then caught a derisive glance and shrugged. 'Oh, well—hey, Joe, could I have your autograph? I've got one of your albums upstairs. Could you sign it for me?'

Joe considered him, gleaming mockery in his stare. 'And then you'll auction it among the girls in your class, I guess?'

'Who, me?' Bobby said hurriedly, a butter-wouldn't-melt-in-my-mouth smile assumed as he gazed back.

'Of course, that would never enter your head, would it?' Joe teased, and Bobby grinned. 'I get the impression you're a guy worth watching,' Joe added, and Bobby looked distinctly flattered. He hurried to do some flattering in his turn.

'You're dead popular with the girls, they swoon when they hear you sing.' He rolled his eyes up and put on a dying expression. 'And they scream,' he added, letting out an eldritch shriek which made Quincy jump. 'Like that,' Bobby explained to Joe. 'They're idiots.'

'How could I refuse such flattery?' Joe shrugged.

Bobby beamed. 'Will you autograph my album?'

'Sure, why not?'

'Thanks,' said Bobby, and took the stairs three at a time, his feet thudding so hard the hall rocked with the sound.

It wasn't until he had gone that Quincy realised she was alone with Joe Aldonez. She began quietly edging towards the sitting-room door again and Joe asked: 'Where are you going?' in a voice which made her halt mid-step and look at him in alarm. He was using that voice which made her hair stand up on the back of her neck; the deep, soft, husky voice which he used when he was singing. He hadn't used it when he talked to Bobby, then he had sounded more brisk.

'I want to know what's going on in there,' she said.

'You'll find out in due course,' he informed her, taking hold of her arm. 'Why don't we make that coffee?'

'Why don't you let go of me?' Quincy retorted, but the cool fingers clamped on her arm gave her no opportunity to evade the steering grip which was leading her towards the kitchen, and she decided it would be undignified to struggle. She already felt she had been made to look ridiculous by this man. Her temper was ready to take off like a rocket to the moon, and Quincy had learnt to be careful about letting her temper slip the leash. She hadn't inherited the red hair which her father's mother had passed on to both Bobby and their elder sister, Lilli, but Quincy had been handed her grandmother's redhot temper. She usually kept it under control—little in her life had ever given her cause to get really angry. The last time she had lost her temper was when she saw some boys throwing stones at a stray dog, and on that occasion she had thrown one of them into the village duckpond. When Quincy did lose her temper she was apt to go too far, as her mother had remarked.

Joe let go of her in the kitchen and she quietly set about making a pot of coffee, ignoring him as he helped by tracking down the cups and getting out the sugar bowl.

'Is Quincy your real name?' he asked, and she nodded.

'What do you do, Quincy? What's your job?'

'I work for my father, I'm his receptionist and I do the typing.'

'Your father's a vet, isn't he?'

She nodded and Joe said: 'When I was a kid I used to dream about being a vet—I was crazy about horses, I'd have given anything to work with them all day. I've got a whole stableful of them now, but I never seem to get time to ride.'

'I used to ride all the time when I was at school,' said Quincy, and a smile came into his dark eyes.

'But not any more? What do you do in your spare time these days, Quincy?' The intimate note in his voice made her stiffen. He was flirting with her and that charm was probably as synthetic as Carmen Lister's smile. He needn't think he could turn it in her direction just because he had nothing more interesting in view. Quincy was under no illusion about her own looks—her face was unlikely to stop any man in his tracks, she was slightly too thin and her short chestnut hair only took on a vivid colour in strong sunlight, when it acquired a golden glint. When she smiled, somehow people always seemed to smile back, though, and she had long ago learnt to live with her own ordinary appearance. Since she only saw herself in mirrors she was unaware of the fact that when she was looking at someone else, her face was vitally alive, heart-shaped, smooth-skinned, her green eyes full of warmth, her pink mouth a tender, gentle curve even in repose.

Ignoring his question, she said: 'I'm sorry Bobby put my name on that competition entry, Mr Aldonez. I realise it must have caused a lot of trouble for you and your publicity people and I apologise, but I couldn't possibly go through with it. I would never have dreamed of entering. I'm not one of your fans, I'm afraid. I wouldn't want to deprive one of them of her dream-come-true.'

'Why are you so cross?' he asked.

'I'm not cross!' she denied.

'Your green eyes have got mad lights in them,' he remarked, staring down into them.

'Oh, I'm crazy now, am I?' she said indignantly, and he laughed.

'Not that sort of crazy—mad as in angry, and getting angrier by the minute.'

'Are you surprised? If anyone around here is crazy it's you and your friends!'

His mouth twisted drily. 'The competition? Hell, that wasn't my idea—Carmen and Billy hatched that between them as publicity for my tour of England. I didn't even know about it until I arrived two days ago—they sprang it on me and it was too late for me to call a halt. I can't attend to every little detail myself, that's Billy's province. He'd sell his own grandmother to get some free publicity.'

'I can believe that,' said Quincy, thinking of the pale, unreadable face of Billy Griffith. She wouldn't trust him further than she could see him—and even then she would watch him like a hawk.

'So you're not one of my fans?' he asked, looking amused as she flushed and glanced away.

'I don't get much time to listen to records,' Quincy evaded, thinking guiltily of the album she had hidden upstairs in her bedroom. She had been playing it endlessly for days, but he wasn't to know that, and she certainly did not intend to pander to his vanity by telling him as much.

'And when you do, I suppose you only listen to classical music?' he enquired, and she saw from the quick look she gave him that he was mocking her again, little teasing glints of gold showing around the fathomless black pupils of those eyes. 'Solid stuff, of course,' he said, pretending to think seriously about it. 'Beethoven or Mozart?'

'Don't put words into my mouth!' she flared, very pink. 'I didn't say anything of the kind. I listen to all sorts of music so long as it's easy on the ear.'

'But I'm not,' he supplied, and she eyed him with wrathful reluctance.

'You know very well you are!' He knew, of course, how could he fail to know? He was one of the top recording stars of America and was beginning to be the most popular male singer over here in England, too, although this was his first big tour of Europe. 'You're . . .' she broke off, biting her lip at his wry smile.

'Go on, Miss Jones,' he mocked. 'I can't wait to hear your verdict.'

'You're not interested in what I think—why should you be?' She was finding his intimate, teasing amusement distinctly nerve-racking, and decided to change the subject. 'I suppose you have to rehearse before your tour starts?'

He did not fail to notice the deliberate introduction of a red herring, but although his eyes gleamed with laughter he answered. 'We kick off in Liverpool in three days' time and go on to some gigs in a couple of other big cities before we go back to London to finish with the big concert.'

'That's sold out, isn't it?' asked Quincy, having read as much in the newspapers. His concerts had been a sell-out within days of the tickets being put on the market and there was a big black market in tickets, she had heard, with people paying fantastic, inflated prices to get hold of one.

Bobby came charging into the room, an album under his arm, and held it out to Joe Aldonez. 'Could you write something across the cover, Joe, not just sign your name?'

Quincy looked at the album furiously—she forgot that she had just told Joe that she didn't like his singing and, her temper soaring, snapped: 'Bobby, you've been in my room again, how many times have I told you to leave my things alone?' Only as she realised what she had said did she stop, her mouth open in a gasp of dismay, meeting the amused gaze of dark eyes and flushing hotly.

'It's yours, is it?' Joe asked softly, watching the colour running up her face with unhidden enjoyment.

'Yeah, it's hers,' Bobby admitted. 'She nearly drove us nuts since she bought it, playing it over and over again.'

It was his most recent album; the record sleeve carrying only a single dark red rose lying against a background of soft black velvet—the image conveying exactly the sexy sound of his voice.

Quincy would have liked to sink down through the floor and never be seen again. She looked at her brother vengefully, and Bobby backed, keeping a wary eye on her. 'But you will autograph it, won't you, Joe?'

'I'd be delighted,' Joe drawled. While they watched he wrote something across the top of the cover, signed his name with a flourish born, Quincy imagined, from autographing a thousand souvenirs, and handed the record back to Bobby, who grinned ear to ear, muttered: 'Thanks, Joe,' and bolted before Quincy could demand her record back. She was dying to know what Joe had written. As soon as he had gone she would pursue Bobby to his lair and retrieve her record before he could auction it or swap it for something he considered more desirable.

The coffee began to make violent noises of impending explosion. She switched it off and Joe took the tray for her through to the sitting-room. She followed, wishing they would all leave. They were visitors from an alien civilisation, as out of place in her quiet little world as she knew she would be in the world they obviously inhabited. Joe might only be wearing black jeans and a white shirt, covered by a black leather jacket fitting tightly at the waist, but she could guess that his clothes were not off the peg: they were designer-made, their cut and fit elegant and sleek. His shirt was silk and clung to that lean, muscled body like a second skin and he breathed an air of sophisticated assurance, wearing the clothes with a casual panache which didn't care what he wore, so certain of himself that she felt he would have looked just as good in shabby, well-washed jeans and an old sweater. Carmen Lister had the same cool, chic certainty about herself.

It wasn't what they wore—it was how they wore it that counted.

Billy Griffith got up as she entered the room and smiled at her. Joe glanced at him, his winged brows lifting in question. 'How are things coming?'

'I've explained how difficult it would be for us to change all the publicity now,' Billy Griffiths said smoothly. 'Mr and Mrs Jones understand the position.' Quincy stared at him and did not much like what she saw. He looked calm and serene, but under his smile he was tempered steel, she sensed, tough and unbreakable, yet ready to bend if he decided it was necessary. Not someone to cross if you could help it, this man, Quincy thought, his charm was strictly skin-deep and his determination to have his own way absolute. As she sat down he sank back into his own chair and leaned towards her.

'Quincy, we're going to have to throw ourselves on your mercy,' he said, smiling. 'Okay, we jumped the gun, and maybe we shouldn't have announced your name to the press before we'd spoken to you, but how were we to guess there'd been this sort of mix-up? We had the draw this afternoon in London, Joe himself picked you out and the press were there at the time. It seemed a great idea to drive down here and have them around when you heard the news. We took your entry at face value.' He smiled again. 'And a very pretty face it is, too—you don't mind my saying that, Quincy? As soon as we saw the photo, we all said: this is our girl!'

'Photo?' Quincy asked, frowning.

Joe put a hand into the pocket of his leather jacket and pulled out a small, crumpled snapshot. She looked at it, appalled.

'Oh, no, Bobby didn't send you that!' It was a very

old photograph of herself in jeans and a cotton T-shirt, the dogs cavorting around her, her chestnut hair blown around her heart-shaped face in wild disorder, her eyes wide and bright as she laughed into the camera. 'That was taken years ago, I'd only just left school!'

'You haven't changed,' Joe assured her, and she looked at him with dislike.

'Thank you!'

'You were just what we were looking for,' Billy Griffiths told her. 'A typical fan, someone to represent all of Joe's millions of fans around the world. You're going to live out the dreams of a million women, Quincy.'

Quincy opened and shut her mouth in an attempt to speak, but she was so angry her voice had gone on strike, she couldn't get a word out, and while she was still in her dumbstruck state, Billy Griffiths said: 'Sit down next to Quincy, Joe, I'm sure she's dying to know what we've got in store for her.'

You bet I am, Quincy thought, wondering if she should escape now and lock herself in her bedroom, or wait until these steamrollers in human form had departed before announcing that she was not going through with whatever horrific plans they had up their sleeves.

Mrs Jones poured the coffee and handed round the cups. Joe sat down and glanced sideways at Quincy, his long lashes sweeping against his tanned skin. 'The general idea is for you to come up to London, have your hair done and buy an evening dress . . .'

'From one of the best new designers,' interrupted Carmen. 'Of course, it will be off the peg. We won't have time to have a dress made for you, but it will be one of a limited range of boutique designs.'

'And you'll go to an exclusive Mayfair beauty salon,' Billy Griffith added.

'You'll be staying with me,' Carmen told her. 'I've got a spare bedroom in my flat. Your parents needn't be anxious about you, you'll be well protected.'

'I don't need a baby-sitter,' Quincy flared. 'How old do you think I am?' If they had been judging by that old photo, they had presumably decided she was in her teens, but surely it must have dawned on them by now that she was older than that?

'Twenty?' Billy Griffith suggested, and she suspected he would have liked her to agree, but she looked him straight in the eye and said firmly that she was twenty-two. He gave a little shrug and murmured something that sounded remarkably like: 'Pity,' but since it was a comment made mostly to himself she couldn't be certain. She could be certain that they would have liked her to be a dewy-eyed schoolgirl, especially when Billy Griffith turned to Mrs Jones and said: 'But she looks pretty young.'

Everyone considered her and Quincy sat there, bristling, which brought a lazy smile curling around Joe's lips.

'You see, Mrs Jones,' Billy went on, ignoring Quincy, having obviously decided that she wasn't sympathetic enough, 'we wanted to find an ordinary girl; someone Joe's fans could identify with, a girl with a happy family background like yours. If we searched for years we couldn't find anyone who looked as perfect as Quincy.'

'Well, you're going to have to,' Quincy told him. 'I'm not going to do it.' Her green eyes flashed angrily. 'I don't want any part of this phoney set-up, I couldn't pretend to swoon and look starry-eyed every time I saw him.'

'Don't worry,' Joe murmured in lazy amusement, 'your first reaction was just what Billy wanted.'

Quincy caught her breath, aghast at the memory of how she must have looked, wide-eyed and open-mouthed, as she first saw him standing outside the front door.

'Absolutely on target,' Billy Griffith agreed complacently. 'That kiss was beautiful stuff, Joe.'

Oh, no, Quincy wailed inwardly—she had been too distraught at the time to think of all those photographs; the kiss itself had been too spellbinding and unbelievable, making her forget everything but the way Joe Aldonez was holding her, but now it dawned on her that it had all been a carefully staged scene in which she was unwittingly playing a leading role, and tomorrow pictures of her in his arms were going to be splashed all over the newspapers.

'You look like a firework getting ready to explode,' Joe said with mockery, and Quincy's furious eyes sparked green flames at him.

'I think the whole business is despicable! I won't do it, and you can't make me.'

'It *was* Bobby who caused all this trouble, Quincy,' Mrs Jones intervened. 'If he hadn't put your name on that form this wouldn't have happened.'

Quincy looked mutinous. 'They should have checked before they announced my name!'

'Even admitting that,' said Joe, 'This is no time to cry over spilt milk. We have to play the game the way the cards have fallen.'

'You may have to,' Quincy told him. 'I don't.'

'If we had to admit what a muddle we'd made of it, we'd be a laughing-stock,' Carmen Lister said tightly.

'What's done is done. The only thing we can do is carry on as though nothing was wrong. As your mother said, your brother got us into this mess. You owe us a favour. What's the problem, anyway? You'll get a trip to London out of it, you'll have an expensive visit to a beauty salon and a new dress, and on top of that you'll have a night out with Joe at one of the best restaurants in London, followed by a visit to a nightclub. Most girls would give their eye teeth for a chance like this.'

'I'm not most girls,' retorted Quincy, and got a long stare of icy dislike from Carmen's blue eyes, the other girl's expression holding such antagonism that despite her dislike of Billy Griffith, Quincy decided that the female was certainly deadlier than the male, at least as far as present company were concerned.

Billy Griffith got up suddenly. 'We must be going,' he said, and smiled at Mr and Mrs Jones. 'It's been very pleasant meeting with you, I hope we'll see each other again.'

They looked surprised as they hurriedly got to their feet, and Carmen Lister stared in disbelief at the manager. He conferred one of his smooth plastic smiles on her. 'Coming, Carmen?'

She clearly had not intended to, Carmen Lister had not yet got her own way with Quincy and she was not the sort of girl who accepted defeat, but Billy Griffith bent and lifted her to her feet, a hand under her elbow. 'You've got a fine show of spring flowers, Mr Jones,' he said, as he steered Carmen towards the door. 'I'd surely like to take a closer look at them—are you a serious gardener?'

'When I've got the time,' said Robert Jones, following. 'Would you like to walk round the garden? You won't see much at this time of the evening.'

'The scent of the daffodils is beautiful at night, though,' Mrs Jones told him as they went out of the door.

Carmen looked back, her brows together, and Billy Griffiths murmured something to her, something Quincy did not catch. The next moment the door had closed and Quincy looked at Joe Aldonez in sudden suspicion—they had left him behind, and she guessed now that that was deliberate, it was why Billy Griffith had so abruptly departed.

Joe turned to face her, one arm along the back of the couch, his eyes meeting hers. 'Okay, Quincy, let me lay it on the line—we need your co-operation. Billy already gave you a big build-up to the press as being a big fan of mine and we'd look pretty silly if you backed out now. I realise it's an embarrassing prospect—publicity stunts are always damned silly. But we're stuck with this one now. Will you go along with it as a favour?'

Quincy stared at him, hesitating. 'I don't know if I could face it, it sounds ghastly, I'd feel a fool.'

'You'll get over that,' he said coolly. 'It will be a nine days' wonder, believe me, the press have very short memories and so have the public. They'll forget it long before you do, but we would be very grateful if you would go through with it.' He paused, frowning. 'Suppose Bobby gets his radio, would that persuade you? That's what he entered for, after all. I guarantee he'll get the biggest and best transistor on the market. How's that?'

'Bribery and corruption!' Quincy accused.

'Bribery,' he admitted wryly, smiling. 'I didn't say anything about corruption—none was offered, none was intended.'

'Well, that's a relief,' she said, and he held out his hand.

'Is it a deal?'

She considered both his suggestion and his hand for a few seconds, then accepted both with a faint sigh. 'It's a deal.'

He released her hand and stood up, his lean body uncoiling gracefully until he towered above her, that black head almost seeming to touch the ceiling as she looked up at him.

'I'll go and put Billy out of his misery,' he said, moving towards the door.

'He left you here deliberately,' Quincy accused, and over his shoulder Joe grinned at her with shameless amusement.

'Obvious, wasn't he? He has great faith in my ability to persuade the opposite sex to do what he wants it to do.'

'How touching,' Quincy said coldly, and he laughed as he went out of the door. Quincy stayed where she was, thinking that, despite Billy Griffith's steely charm and unreal smiles, it was Joe Aldonez who was the dangerous one of the two—and Billy Griffith clearly knew it. Now Quincy knew it, too, and she would not forget it. Forewarned is forearmed, she told herself, as she heard her parents outside saying goodbye and then the sound of a car moving purringly away in the spring night.

CHAPTER TWO

HER parents were very late leaving for their dinner date, and left in an excited flurry, reminding Quincy to ring the restaurant and warn them that Mr and Mrs Jones would be an hour later than they had planned. Quincy made the call, then went into the kitchen to start getting supper for herself and Bobby. The idea of macaroni cheese no longer held such great appeal, she decided, holding the fridge door open and staring indifferently at the assembled contents. The easiest thing to make would be a cheese omelette, so she collected a carton of eggs and some cheese.

While she was whisking the eggs, Brendan appeared in the doorway, hovering uncertainly and watching her as though he had never seen her before.

'Hi,' she said, then remembered asking him to supper. 'Oh, have you come for your macaroni cheese, because if you have it's cheese omelette, do you still want some?'

He frowned but nodded. 'Thanks, that sounds fine.'

Quincy dropped some butter in the pan and watched it melt. Brendan leaned against the wall, his eyes on her, but Quincy's thoughts were elsewhere, she was barely conscious that he was in the room.

'I don't think it's a good idea,' Brendan said suddenly in a flat voice, and she glanced round, starting.

'Don't you? I'm sorry, I just went off the idea of macaroni cheese—how would you like some soup instead?'

'Not the supper,' he said in an impatient voice, his brows knitted. 'This idea of going up to London!'

She felt her cheeks glowing, and turned her head away quickly. 'Oh, that!'

'You'll be out of your element,' Brendan said roughly. 'You're not that sort of girl.'

Indignant, Quincy asked crossly: 'What sort of girl is that? Good heavens, all that will happen is that I'll be taken out to dinner by Joe Aldonez—they aren't planning anything more lethal than caviar and champagne for two.' Having said that she felt herself drifting back into the half-dream which had been engrossing her, her mind's eye picturing how it would be, and Brendan gave an irritated little snort.

'It's started already, hasn't it?'

'What has?' the butter had begun to smoke and change colour and Quincy hurriedly poured the whisked egg into the pan.

'That kiss,' said Brendan in tones of disgust.

Quincy bent her head, her face very flushed, and attended to the half-cooked omelette, folding it neatly so that the softly melting grated cheese could continue to cook inside the perfect semi-circle of golden egg.

'You don't want to get involved with people like that,' Brendan informed her. 'Don't you realise what sort of life he must lead?'

Quincy had realised exactly what sort of life a top singing star must lead. She had read gossip items and stories in magazines about girls throwing themselves at their idols and she had no intention of getting involved with Joe Aldonez, but for some peculiar reason she found it very annoying to have Brendan giving her a gypsy's warning. Ignoring what he was saying, she tipped the cooked omelette out of the pan on to a warmed dish, and slid it into the warming compartment of the oven while she turned to cook another one.

'Listen to me, Quincy,' said Brendan, shifting on his feet in a baulked, frustrated way. 'You're a very innocent girl, you know.'

'How dare you?' Quincy flared, turning on him, her eyes as green as an angry cat's. 'Who are you insulting? Don't you talk about me as if I was ten years old!'

'I'm not insulting you,' Brendan protested in aghast tones, staring at her furious face. 'What's wrong with you? I only want to protect you—you don't realise what could happen to you, what you could get yourself into!'

Quincy's teeth met and she went on cooking omelettes, her head averted.

'He's a sophisticated man,' Brendan told her. 'You're just another girl to him. He must have had girls all over the world by now. You only have to look at him to see what sort of morals he's got.' His voice held distaste and contempt. 'For him, you'll just be another one-night stand, Quincy, but you could get hurt, and I don't want that.'

She switched off the heat as she finished her cooking and turned to give Brendan a quick, contrite smile. He meant well and she was fond of him, it was stupid of her to get annoyed because he was trying to save her from getting hurt. How was he to guess that he had been damaging her ego when he pointed out how innocent she was—Brendan couldn't guess he was touching on a sore point. Quincy had not realised how cosy and protected, how innocent and peaceful, her world was until tonight, when Joe Aldonez and his entourage erupted into it to break up their halcyon serenity. Everything that had happened, everything that had been said about her by Billy Griffith and Carmen Lister, had given her a new image of herself. They saw her as a wide-eyed, unsophisticated country mouse who idolised Joe Aldonez from a distance and no doubt Joe Aldonez himself saw her the same way. Quincy felt that realisation inside herself like a poisoned thorn under her skin. She did not want Joe Aldonez looking at her with amused, mocking eyes. She did not want him to tease and torment her because he thought her lack of worldly sophistication something to smile about.

'I can take care of myself,' she told Brendan, assuming a calm confidence she did not feel. 'Don't you worry about me! I'm only going because they promised to give Bobby a transistor for his birthday—I'm in no danger from Joe Aldonez, you can be sure of that.'

Brendan did not look very convinced. He stared at her flushed face, then clumsily grabbed her shoulders and kissed her hard. Quincy jerked in surprise, eyes wide open. Brendan let go and stood back, brick red.

'Just don't let them change you,' he muttered. 'I like you just the way you are!' He walked away, saying, 'I'll call Bobby, shall I?'

Quincy couldn't think of anything to say—it wasn't the first time Brendan had kissed her. They had been dancing together, had a few dates, but somehow although they were always at ease together there had never been that special, tingling excitement between them which she instinctively knew came with a genuine attraction. She liked Brendan, but she was far from falling in love with him. She knew him too well, he was always there, always the same; a part of her life like the

wallpaper or the sound of the dogs barking in the
garden. When love came, she had long ago decided, it
ought to come like the sudden shock of a collision with
the unknown, sending electricity sparking through the
veins. Only today she had been telling herself that that
was all romantic folly—love mostly came more quietly.
After all, you were choosing a man for life, and one
instant of dazzling sexual attraction was no basis for
such a lifetime's decision. She might give herself wise
advice on the subject, but how did you get yourself to
listen?

Brendan was very quiet over supper. Bobby more
than made up for that—he chattered non-stop as he
ate, excited by what had happened.

'Wait till I get to school tomorrow—boy, are my pals
going to be green with envy!'

'I want my album back,' Quincy told him sternly.
'You aren't swapping it for anything, Bobby Jones,
don't think you are! That album is mine, remember,
and don't you ever go hunting around my room again,
keep out of it, you hear?'

He made an unabashed face at her. 'Who was in my
room today, then? If you can, I can.'

She gave an indignant snort. 'I was trying to tidy
your room for Mum—I don't know how you can bear
to live in it, it looks like the local garbage tip.'

'At least I don't hide anything,' Bobby jeered. 'I
heard you lying to Joe—telling him you didn't like his
singing when you've been sitting around for weeks all
starry-eyed listening to that album.'

Quincy was about to fly at him, descending to his
level, when she remembered Brendan and felt him
staring at her. She gave Bobby a sweet, forgiving
sisterly smile of ineffable condescension.

'Time little boys were in bed, isn't it?' she asked.

Bobby glared. 'Very funny,' he snapped, but got up, all the same. 'I was going, anyway,' he told her.

It was not until she was in bed herself several hours later that it dawned on her that Bobby had successfully evaded her attempt to get her record back. She would have to catch him in the morning, she told herself, turning over on to her side.

What had Joe Aldonez written on it? Lying in the dark she remembered the way those thick black lashes had flickered against his cheek as he wrote across the record sleeve. A wicked little smile had curled his hard lips upwards. What had been in his mind?

She had to face the fact that she was unlikely ever to find out anything of the man but his sexy, smouldering public image—that was what he was always careful to project, she supposed. He had to be seen the way his fans wanted to see him. What was he like behind that, though?

She found it hard to get to sleep that night, and when she woke up it was broad daylight, the spring sunshine dancing on the ceiling of her bedroom and the garden alive with the call of birds, the shadow of their wings flitting past the window now and then as she lay watching, struggling to surface from the depths of sleep.

Her head felt heavy, she had a vague memory of strange dreams, but the strangest of them was lingering with her as she glanced at the clock. Had it been a dream? Or had Joe Aldonez really burst into her life last night?

'Aren't you awake yet?' Her mother came into the room with a cup of tea, shaking her head. 'You have to be ready at nine, remember.'

'Ready?' repeated Quincy dazedly, sitting up.

'They're coming to pick you up,' Mrs Jones reminded her, drawing the curtains. 'Shall I pack for you while you get ready?'

'Oh,' Quincy murmured, speechless, the cup trembling in her hands and almost spilling hot tea over the bed. It was no dream—it had all happened. 'I can't go,' she burst out. 'Mum, I can't!'

Mrs Jones laughed. 'Of course you can, you'll have fun in London. Mr Griffith promised your father you would be perfectly safe with them, the last thing they would want was any trouble, this is a very important publicity stunt.'

'What about Dad?' Quincy asked. 'Who'll do my job while I'm away? You know how the paperwork piles up, and somebody has to answer the phone when Dad and Brendan are out on their rounds.'

'I'll do that,' her mother assured her. 'Who do you think did it before you took over? I can do it with one hand tied behind my back.'

Quincy looked at her mother helplessly, seeing the excitement brightening her eyes. Mrs Jones was loving the situation—nothing like this had ever happened in their lives before.

'Your father just went down to get all the newspapers,' Mrs Jones told her. 'I wonder if Lilli is back in London yet? I'll give her a ring later.'

'Mum,' Quincy started to say, feeling shivery and faintly sick, and then the phone began to ring downstairs and her mother gave a little groan.

'I'd better answer that as your father's out.' She bustled out of the room and went downstairs. Quincy slowly drank her tea. She wasn't hungry this morning; her mind was in too confused a state.

She put down the cup and reluctantly got out of bed just as her mother reappeared. 'That was Lilli,' Mrs Jones told her eagerly, all smiles. 'She just read the morning paper and couldn't believe her eyes. She says you must stay with her while you're in London, it would be silly for you to stay with that editor when your own sister can look after you.'

Quincy felt a surge of relief. 'Oh, that would be a good idea!' If she was staying with Lilli she would have a safe refuge where the insanity of Joe Aldonez' world couldn't touch her. 'I'd much prefer that,' she said.

'I thought you would,' her mother nodded. 'Go and have your bath, while I pack a case for you. They'll be here in half an hour.'

Quincy hesitated over what to wear. Her wardrobe was hardly in the high fashion class, she relied heavily on jeans and sweaters. In bra and panties she stood in front of the mirror, gloomily considering her clothes, and finally took down a camelhair skirt which Lilli had given her last Christmas. It had been expensive, Quincy suspected, Lilli's clothes usually were, but her career demanded she constantly buy new ones and she sometimes passed on to Quincy some garment she was tired of or had decided was not suitable for the job.

Slipping into a jade-green sweater, also a gift from Lilli, Quincy studied herself ruefully. She looked just what she was—a country mouse about to venture up to town.

She brushed her hair until it gleamed, golden lights among the rich chestnut strands, and took care over her make-up, outlining her lips with a warm pink and brushing pale green eye-shadow across her lids.

The finished result was hardly going to set the world

on fire—and would certainly not set Joe Aldonez on fire, Quincy thought, then bit her lip, angry with herself. Who wants to set him on fire? she asked her reflection crossly. Are you crazy? Will you stop thinking like that?

Her green eyes flashed back at her like exploding fireworks as she turned hurriedly away. Her mind was in a state of total insanity, she admitted. It wasn't so surprising, the last twenty-four hours had been enough to turn any sane girl into a gibbering idiot, but Quincy was not prepared to forgive herself for letting her head whirl over a man who was only using her to get himself some big publicity.

From downstairs her mother's voice called frantically: 'He's here! Quincy, he's here!'

He? Quincy thought, jumping about six feet into the air, her nerves jangling. Who does she mean? Not him, not Joe Aldonez, surely? He wouldn't have come himself! She had imagined he would send a chauffeur or possibly that dreadful Billy Griffith.

She ran to the window but was too late to see who had arrived. A gleaming white Ferrari sports car was parked outside the house, but whoever had been driving it had been admitted downstairs, she heard her mother talking in excited tones.

'Quincy!' her mother called up the stairs. 'Aren't you ready yet, darling?'

'Coming!' Quincy called back, her voice low and husky. She took a final, nervous look at herself in the mirror. Who was that strange girl staring back at her with huge, glazed, bright green eyes, her skin a hectic colour and her mouth not quite steady?

She walked down the stairs, carrying the picture with her, unreality settling around her like a brittle shell, sealing her off from the true impact of what was happening to her.

Joe Aldonez stood in the hall with her mother. His eyes lifted to drift over Quincy as she came down towards them, and if it had not been for the protective shell she had managed to seal around herself she might have turned tail and bolted from him in trepidation, but, wearing a stiff set smile, she went on down the stairs, her head lifted, moving as gracefully as she could on legs that trembled.

'Here she is,' Mrs Jones said triumphantly, as though Quincy was making some grand entrance.

'So I see,' Joe Aldonez drawled as Quincy looked at him, her eyes dazzled by the sun shining into them, seeing him through a vivid halo of dancing light. 'I've put your case in the car,' he added. 'Are you ready?'

'Mr Aldonez is going to drive you there himself,' her mother pointed out.

'Joe,' he urged, turning his quick, warm smile towards Mrs Jones. 'Everyone just calls me Joe, except my mother.'

'What does she call you?' Quincy asked with a dryness she hadn't intended, surprised for some peculiar reason at the idea that he had parents like everyone else. There was something so different about him, a special magic centred on his name, which seemed to set him apart from the rest of the human race. Every time she saw him she felt a jab of disbelief.

He had turned his glance back to her, those eyes of his glittering jet beneath his winged brows. 'José,' he said. 'That's what I was baptised.'

'That's Spanish,' Mrs Jones said curiously.

He nodded. 'My mother is Spanish and my father is of Spanish descent although he was born in California.'

He grinned, a rakish amusement in his face. 'So was his father,' he added. 'My family came to the States a hundred years ago. I'm a fourth generation American.'

'Have you ever been to Spain?' asked Mrs Jones, and he shook his head.

'But I mean to try to see some of it while I'm over here in Europe,' he told her. 'I've promised my mother I'll visit her family if I get time. She was over there last year, but I was too busy to go with her.'

'Does she live in California?' Quincy asked.

He nodded. 'My family have some orange groves there—the land has been in the family for over fifty years. My grandfather bought it during the Depression.' His eyes danced. 'He won some money in a poker game and he'd have lost it the same way, if my grandmother hadn't taken it out of his pocket when he was asleep and hidden it. She talked him into buying the land before she told him where the money was—a very determined woman, my grandmother.'

Quincy was fascinated and could have gone on asking questions, hoping by his answers to make herself believe he was real and not some dark fantasy conjured up from her own imagination, but he looked at his watch and said: 'Time to get moving, I'm afraid.' Holding out his hand, he smiled at Mrs Jones. 'Nice to know you, Mrs Jones—I'll look forward to seeing you again real soon.'

Fluttered and flushed, Mrs Jones followed them to the door and stood there, waving, as he put Quincy into the passenger seat of the sleek sports car. Quincy looked back at her mother with a drowning sense of alarmed dismay. Mrs Jones waved vigorously as the engine fired and the car drew smoothly away from the house, putting on speed at once, the elegant lines of

the vehicle built for the race track as much as for the
busy roads, taking them shooting past every other car
without effort.

Joe glanced sideways at her, his brows meeting. 'Do
up your seat-belt.'

Something in the cool arrogance of the tone made
her sit up, bristling. She obeyed, but gave him a look
which brought another of those glinting little smiles
her way.

'Feeling belligerent this morning, are we?' he asked
in a soft, taunting voice. 'I had the feeling you were
when you came downstairs. Had some second thoughts
about coming to London?'

'I don't know why I ever agreed,' she admitted,
hurling the words at him like little sharpened flints.

'Too late to change your mind now,' he said, putting
on even more speed as he hit the motorway going to
London, the beautiful streamlined car flashing along
the fast lane while every other driver gazed in envious
reverence at it as it passed them.

'You know I'm going to stay with my sister, not
with Miss Lister?' asked Quincy, her chestnut curls
fluttering around her face in the slipstream of cold air
blowing around her.

'Your mother mentioned it,' he agreed. 'She said
your sister was a dancer—what sort of dancer is she?'

'She's part of a dance group who appear on television
and who do cabaret now and then—they're called The
Panthers.' The family were very proud of Lilli, she
was the nearest approach to a star they had known
before Joe Aldonez erupted into their lives.

'How many dancers in the group?' Joe asked.

'Fifteen,' said Quincy, realising he had never heard
of her sister's act. Lilli wasn't in the superstar bracket,

of course, but maybe one day she would be—she was very beautiful and talented. Quincy wondered suddenly, with a funny little twist of dismay inside her, what Joe Aldonez would think of Lilli. Every other man Quincy had ever met—apart from Brendan—had fallen for Lilli on sight, bewitched by her fiery hair and lovely face. Quincy secretly viewed the man beside her through her lowered lashes. Would he fall for Lilli, too? What if he does? she asked herself impatiently—what difference would it make to you, you idiot? He's flashed into your life like a comet and he'll flash out again in a few days.

They slowed as they met an incoming stream of traffic and someone in another car stared, open-mouthed, at Joe Aldonez. Quincy saw his involuntary grimace as he realised he had been recognised. The white Ferrari roared away, leaving the much slower car behind, and Joe leaned forward to open the glove compartment in front of him. Quincy watched him take out some dark glasses and slip them on, their mirror lenses completely hiding those eyes of his. His lean, tanned face took on a new air, making it far less likely anyone would recognise him now.

'Where did you stay last night?' she asked him, and he turned, the lenses flashing blankly in her direction.

'We all went off to a hotel in Bath,' he said. 'Carmen and Billy drove back to London a couple of hours ago.'

'Why did you come to pick me up?' she asked, and saw his brows lift at the question, adding hurriedly: 'I thought you'd send someone.'

'I was driving back, anyway,' he drawled. With those dark glasses on she had no idea whether he was smiling or not, his mouth had a curve even in repose which was misleading.

'Aren't you worried that someone will recognise you?' she asked and he grinned.

'In this case they would need to have wings to catch up with me!'

Quincy looked around at the soft white velvety leather upholstery, the gleaming chrome of the dashboard. 'It's a beautiful car.'

'I like cars,' he said. 'The faster the better,' and put on yet more speed, sending her heart into her mouth.

'I don't like driving fast!' she gasped, clutching the edge of her seat as she swayed with the car. 'Slow down! The speed limit is only seventy miles an hour over here.'

He slowed, giving her a teasing look. 'I'd forgotten— I don't want to get picked up for speeding, do I? Now that wouldn't be good publicity?'

'Is that all you ever think about?' she accused.

'I've had to learn that I'm a public figure,' Joe told her with a wry intonation, shrugging. This morning he was still wearing that black leather jacket, but the shirt under it was black silk today. It hugged his muscled body just as smoothly, the collar open, giving her a glimpse of his strong brown throat. She wondered idly if that tan was habitual, did he do a lot of sunbathing in California? His face, hands, neck were a uniform golden-brown—did the rest of his body match? A sudden wave of heated colour spread up her face as she realised what she was doing—imagining him without the expensive silk shirt and the tight-fitting jeans. Her mind really had gone haywire, she scolded herself, averting her eyes. What was the matter with her?

'Want some music?' he asked, leaning forward again to switch on the car radio. They didn't talk for a while,

driving so fast that they ate up the miles to London
without Quincy being aware how far they had gone.
On the motorway the countryside looked so similar
wherever you were—just green fields and cows and
dreaming elm trees on either side with the white concrete ribbon of road unwinding in front of you.

When one of his own records came on, Joe gave a
little groan and put out a hand to flick the radio off.
'No, thanks,' he said under his breath.

'Don't you like to hear yourself sing?' That idea had
never occurred to her.

'By the time an album is released, I'm sick to death
of hearing myself,' he confessed drily. 'First you have
hours of rehearsing, then hours of recording and re-
recording—I find I've lost the ability to hear a song by
the time I've sung it a hundred times. I never listen to
my own recordings, only ever those of somebody else.'

'How did you get into the music business?'

'By accident,' he said. 'I was singing at a party,
someone heard me—and next thing I knew I was sign-
ing a contract. Once upon a time singing was fun—
now it's my job.' He turned his head, black hair blowing wildly around his tanned face. 'If you have illusions
about the business, forget them. I work very hard, for
very long hours. I used to escape from work on my
father's orange trees to sing—now I try to escape from
singing to give Dad a hand.'

Quincy listened, frowning. He was altering her
whole idea of the sort of life he led. Was he being
honest?

'How often do you go home to see your family?' she
asked, and he shrugged.

'Not as often as I'd like—it's the only place in the
world where I can be myself without being watched.

The older I get, the more I value my home. I'm very lucky. My parents haven't changed an inch. My mother will still give me a tongue-lashing if she thinks I need it.' His sideways smile was mocking. 'You should meet her, I've a feeling you two would get on like a house on fire.' He looked back at the busy road. 'She's a very real woman, too.'

Quincy was taken aback by that remark, flattered by it despite her inner resolve to remain untouched by anything he said.

They made London inside three hours and would have got there earlier if the traffic had not thickened as they approached the capital, and slowed the white Ferrari down.

'Lilli lives in Chelsea,' Quincy said as they fought their way into the inner city.

'Would you mind if we call in at my hotel first?' he asked, glancing at her. 'Carmen will be waiting there for us and I'd better let her know you won't be sharing her flat. A change of arrangements could annoy her, I warn you.'

'I'm sorry, but I'd rather stay with my sister,' Quincy said, and he shrugged, his face not easy to read.

She was not looking forward to confronting Carmen Lister—the other girl had made a very unfavourable impression when they met. Quincy felt herself tightening up inside as she followed Joe into the hushed environment of one of London's most exclusive hotels. He looked at her, taking off his dark glasses, and began to smile as he absorbed the defiant flush on her face.

'Getting ready to do battle?' he mocked. 'Think you can take Carmen on, do you? She's a tough lady.'

He collected his key at the desk and walked along

the carpeted gallery to the lift. Quincy stood beside him as it rose smoothly, her eyes avoiding the betraying reflection of herself in the mirror-lined walls. She did not need to see herself to know that her green eyes were hectic, her face taut. What could Carmen Lister do to her, anyway? she asked herself. Quincy did not enjoy arguments, but she had no intention of backing down on this one. She would feel much happier if she was staying with Lilli, and Carmen Lister was not talking her out of it.

Joe had a large suite overlooking one of London's royal parks, and, as they let themselves into it he called out: 'Billy? We're here!'

There was no answer, the rooms lay silent and, apparently, empty, in the spring sunshine. Joe walked ahead into a spacious, beautifully furnished sitting-room and stood there, twirling the doorkey on one finger as he looked around.

Arrangements of spring flowers stood around the room; blue iris in velvety sprays, daffodils and delicate white narcissus, their scent filling the air. A white envelope was propped against one vase. Joe walked over and picked it up, pulled out a sheet of paper and read it with a slight frown. Quincy stood nervously near the door, feeling shy and out of place in the luxurious surroundings.

Looking up, Joe said wryly: 'They're both otherwise occupied, it seems. Do you want to ring your sister and see if she's home?'

Quincy nodded, relieved not to have to face Carmen Lister after all. She picked up the phone and dialled Lilli's number. There was no reply and slowly she put the phone down. Joe was watching her.

'No answer?'

She shook her head, wondering what to do now. It had not occurred to her that Lilli might not be home.

'Why don't we have lunch up here?' Joe asked. 'I don't know about you, but I'm ready to eat a rare steak.' He picked up the phone and rang room service without waiting for her to answer. 'Steak okay for you, too?' he enquired only after he had dialled the number.

'Yes, thank you,' she said, very politely. There was something about the sunny silence of the large suite which made her uncomfortably aware of being alone with him.

'Medium?' he asked, and she nodded.

'French fried or just salad?' he asked, and she told him salad would be fine.

He ordered for them both, adding a request for a bottle of wine. As he put down the phone he made a little face at her.

'Judging by my previous experience of this hotel that will take them a good half an hour,' he said drily. 'Take off your coat, it's warm in here.'

She unbuttoned her camelhair coat with fingers which were not very steady and Joe took off his leather jacket and flung it over a chair. He moved so lightly that she wasn't aware of it until she felt him right behind her, sliding her coat off her shoulders, his cool fingers brushing lightly against her neck. A shiver ran through her and she involuntarily flinched.

'Don't get uptight,' he said in a brisk voice. 'I'm not about to make a heavy pass.'

'I didn't think you were!' Quincy denied, her face flushing.

'You're lying in your teeth,' he accused, tossing her coat down on top of his jacket, the little movement tightening the fit of that silk shirt, making her very conscious of the powerful lean body under it. He put a finger on the side of her throat where a tiny pulse was beating violently. 'What's that?' he asked, angry mockery in his black eyes. 'Do you think I don't know your heart's going like a steam-hammer?'

'Not for you!' Quincy mumbled incoherently, pulling away. 'You don't make my heart miss a beat, Mr Aldonez. If I'm flushed, it's the central heating in here, it's far too warm.'

'Oh, is that what it is?' he asked in a soft, intimate voice which made her swallow with alarm, taking another step nearer, making Quincy instinctively back even further. Her legs came up against the elegant brocade couch behind her and, off balance, she abruptly sat down on it.

That was a mistake. Joe was sitting beside her a second later, his thigh against her, leaning towards her, his body twisted so that he could look into her startled, alarmed eyes.

'Can you see in the dark?' he asked.

The question baffled her. 'What?' she said, totally at sea. What was he talking about?

'You have eyes like a cat,' he explained. 'As green as grass and full of spitting defiance—I wouldn't like to feel those little claws, I bet they're as sharp as razors.' His fingers curled round one of her hands and lifted it, spread across his palm, the pearly nails gleamed. 'They don't look sharp,' he added, his mouth curving in a smile. 'But I suspect they're as deceptive as the rest of you.'

Quincy looked at him uneasily—he was flirting with her quite deliberately, she was not so innocent that she did not understand that. At such close quarters he was almost hypnotic, a man of sexual magnetism who knew precisely how he could affect a woman when he looked into her eyes, the self-assured glitter of his dark gaze riveting her attention in spite of her common sense. The fact that he had 'dangerous' written all over him merely intensified the threat he exuded. Quincy could not help wondering what it would feel like to be in his arms again, to have that firm, male mouth compelling her lips to submit. When he kissed her the first time she had been too dazed to enjoy the experience—it had happened too fast, too inexplicably. In spite of her determination to be calm and controlled whenever he was around, she had been a prey to helpless fantasies about that kiss, wishing she could run the moment again, like some slow-motion replay.

'Lost your tongue?' he enquired drily when she was silent.

'I wasn't saying anything because I haven't got anything to say,' Quincy threw back crossly, glaring at him.

'There's a novelty,' he mocked. 'A woman who doesn't talk if she hasn't anything to say—you must be unique. I'm surprised you're still wandering around fancy-free—are all the men in your life blind?'

'No,' Quincy said demurely, looking down.

She felt him watching her. 'I didn't think to ask,' he said, in an altered voice. 'Is there someone in your life?'

'What business of yours is that?' she asked, and his fingers closed round her chin, lifting it until he could see her green eyes.

'Is there?' he insisted, then a sudden frown pulled his brows together. 'Now I remember it, there was someone with you last night, wasn't there? When you opened the door I got a vague impression of a guy lurking in the background. I'd forgotten him. Who was it?'

'Brendan,' Quincy said. 'My father's partner.'

'Married?' he asked quickly, and she shook her head. 'How old is he?' Joe demanded.

'Thirty.'

His mouth twisted and he released her. 'And does he harbour ideas of marrying into the practice?' he asked in a light, mocking voice. 'Does he fancy you, Quincy?'

'What if he does?' she asked, something inside her prickling angrily. Had he imagined that she had no boy-friends? Quincy's pride rebelled against the idea that Joe had decided she was unlikely to have other men in her life.

He leaned back, his hands clasped behind his head, the long supple body at rest.

'I suppose it would be very suitable,' he drawled in a dry voice. 'Your parents would approve—they wouldn't be losing a daughter, just acquiring another vet.'

'I don't think that's funny,' Quincy flared. Her temper shot away from her and she added furiously: 'What's the matter, Mr Aldonez? Disappointed to discover I'm not going to be quite the push-over you expected? If you had the idea that I was going to fall into your arms without a qualm, you'd better think again. I've agreed to go through with this ridiculous cheap publicity stunt, but only under pressure. As far as I'm concerned, the sooner this is all over, the better I'll like it. I shan't enjoy pretending to think you're the best thing since sliced bread, I hate telling lies, even when there seems to be no alternative. You should

have hired an actress to play the part of an adoring
fan, she might have done a much better job. I won't
find it quite so easy to pretend.'

Joe had sat listening to her, his face changing, until
by the time she had run out of steam he was staring at
her, no longer a charming, mocking man with teasing
dark eyes, but a man carved out of flint; features hard
and grim, eyes glittering.

CHAPTER THREE

BEFORE he could react, however, someone tapped at
the door of the suite and a moment later the floor
waiter wheeled a laden table into the sitting-room,
bowing to them as he courteously said: 'Good day,
m'sieur, mademoiselle.'

Joe rose with a graceful twist of his lean figure as
the waiter drew two chairs up to the table. Quincy got
up, too, and sat down with the waiter bowing behind
her chair. He flicked out one of the starched damask
napkins and laid it over her lap.

'*Bon appetit,*' he murmured, and she gave him a weak
smile.

When he had gone Joe picked up a glass of the red
wine he had ordered and drank some, his eyes lowered.
The room seemed to Quincy to be heavy with brooding
hostility. She concentrated on her steak, although she
had lost all appetite. Joe ate, too, in silence. Quincy
was bitterly regretting her stupid outburst, but she
could not bring herself to apologise. How could she
explain to him that her anger had been born out of a

miserable sense of her own very ordinary self, her lack of beauty and glamour, compared to the sort of girls he must meet every day? Her pride had wanted to deny that she found him violently attractive—she would rather have him think he left her cold than have him realise she could hardly take her eyes off him when he was in the same room.

He might have been flirting lightly with her, but it had meant nothing, Quincy realised that. Either he had been amusing himself with her—which stung her pride—or he had been going through the motions, acting to keep her happy, making her feel terrific. He was a public performer, after all, he was used to make-believe. It wouldn't be hard for him to use every ounce of that undoubted sex appeal to make her head spin. When he sang he turned it full on like some high-voltage spotlight, his male sensuality throbbing in every husky note. It didn't mean a thing to him, but Quincy was determined not to let herself fall for it. She would only get hurt. She was a small town girl and she took life seriously—she did not need to have a diagram drawn for her to understand that if she took Joe Aldonez seriously she would be in danger of losing her heart.

They had just finished their meal when Carmen Lister and Billy Griffith arrived. Carmen threw a comprehensive glance over the table, lifted her perfectly arched brows in amusement.

'Has Joe been wining and dining you?' she asked Quincy with a smile that stripped Quincy's pride bare, as she read the cynicism, the mockery, in the other woman's face. Perhaps Carmen Lister had had the dazzling spotlight of Joe's charm turned on her some time? Carmen was more able to protect herself than

Quincy, though. Her head was unlikely to be turned by one of his intimate smiles. Carmen Lister's head was screwed on very firmly, Quincy suspected.

Billy Griffith shook hands vigorously. 'Great to see you,' he told her. 'Wonderful—er . . .'

'Quincy,' Joe supplied as the man paused, obviously at a loss to remember her name.

'Sure,' said Billy. 'Quincy—cute name, I like it.' He gave her a nod and turned to Joe. 'Rehearsal three o'clock, Joe, and we get the plane to Liverpool tomorrow at eight-thirty. We're going straight to rehearse at the hall, everything's set up.'

Joe nodded. 'Fine. By the way, Quincy would prefer to stay with her sister while she's in London. Could someone drive her there?'

Carmen frowned. 'Where does your sister live?' she asked Quincy, who told her flatly,

'Chelsea.'

Carmen looked at Billy Griffith. 'I don't think that's a good idea, we ought to have her where we can see her,' she said.

'If that's what she wants, she must do it,' Joe interrupted in a curt voice.

'But, Joe . . .'

'No argument,' he said. 'It will put her at her ease, and it will look better for her to be staying with one of her family rather than with you.'

'That's true,' Billy agreed, and Carmen shrugged.

'Okay,' she said with an irritated frown. 'Just as you say, Joe. Come on, Quincy, I'll drive you there—I ought to meet your sister.'

Billy had wandered away towards the window, but he turned now. 'Is your sister married?' he asked. 'Got any kids?'

'No,' said Quincy, and he turned away, losing interest.

- 'Pity, good human interest there.'

Quincy looked at him with acute dislike. He wasn't a man, he was a money-making machine who cared for nothing but profit and made every single thing in life seem pointless unless it could be useful. She did not envy Joe his life, surrounded by men like that, men for whom everything had to have a commercial motive.

'You'd better ring to check your sister's home,' Joe told her in a quiet voice, and she turned to pick up the phone. This time the ringing was answered and Lilli's voice said: 'Hallo?'

'Lilli, this is Quincy.' Conscious of the others listening to her, Quincy sounded unlike herself, her voice low and breathless.

'Quincy! Where are you? When will you be in London? I can't wait to see you—I'm just so excited, I can't believe this has happened to you, of all people!'

Quincy laughed lightly, glad no one else could hear what Lilli was saying and indignant at the last frank comment. What did Lilli mean? Her of all people? Why shouldn't it have happened to her? The fact that her own reaction had been as incredulous was beside the point, she felt.

'I'm in London,' she said. 'Can I come over now? I've been trying to get in touch with you, but you weren't answering your phone.'

'I was shopping,' Lilli explained. 'Of course you can come now—I'm dying to see you, are you at the station?'

Quincy decided not to tell her she was in Joe Aldonez's suite at a swish London hotel. 'I'll be there in a quarter of an hour,' she said. 'See you soon.'

Joe moved to pick up her coat. Quincy stiffened as he held it, sliding it up her arms. Having him anywhere near her did something drastic to her heartbeat, and that made her angry with herself. What sort of idiot was she?

'I'll be seeing you when I get back from my gigs,' he said behind her in a deep, cool voice, the sound of it iced with a lingering memory of what she had said to him before their lunch arrived.

She nodded and followed Carmen out of the suite. By the time she saw Joe Aldonez again, she told herself sternly, she was going to have herself firmly under control again, her stupid heart obediently keeping its usual regular rhythm and her blood flowing around her body at a sensible speed. He wasn't going to see her blushing and jumping with nerves every time he touched her in future.

'What's the address?' Carmen asked her as the doorman held open the door of the small red car.

Quincy told her and slid into the passenger seat. A moment later they were weaving their way through heavy London traffic, turning south towards the Embankment along the Thames. The spring day was fading softly, the air cool and bright, but the sky a delicate lavender blue over the steel-grey river. Knots of barges passed slowly along the water towards the docks and a yellow-beaked gull screamed as it climbed above the choppy water.

'Your sister works in London, I suppose?' Carmen asked, giving her a brief cold look. Quincy distinctly got the feeling the other girl did not like her much, but Carmen Lister was the sort of girl who made you feel her own sex was not on her wavelength, she was strictly a man's woman; businesslike, tough and independent.

No doubt she used her sexual attraction, of which she probably had a plentiful supply, if she thought it useful, but Quincy could not imagine her losing her head or missing a night's sleep over a man. She talked to Billy Griffith as an equal, which, Quincy felt, was a betraying attitude, and although she smiled at Joe Aldonez with a definite glint in her eyes, Quincy wouldn't like to bet on it that Carmen was any more excited by him than she was by anyone else. Carmen had the hard eyes of a woman with her gaze set on her own future.

'She's a dancer with The Panthers,' Quincy said, and felt Carmen shoot another stare at her.

'Oh, is she?' There was thoughtful assessment behind that remark. 'What do you do, Quincy? I gathered you just helped at home.'

'I'm the receptionist in my father's surgery,' Quincy told her. 'I help my mother in the house, too, when she needs it.'

'A home girl,' Carmen commented, and she wasn't being complimentary, she made it sound like a purring insult. 'Haven't you ever wanted to do something more exciting?'

'No,' Quincy said defiantly. 'I like helping my father—I like animals and I hate to see them in pain, I get satisfaction out of knowing I'm helping them. I can't think of any other job I'd rather do—except be a vet myself, and I wasn't good enough to take the exams. There's too much to learn and it takes years.'

Carmen smiled, kind contempt in her face. 'Well, so long as you're happy,' she dismissed as she pulled up in front of Lilli's flat. Lilli had two small rooms on the ground floor of a narrow Edwardian terraced house several streets away from the river. It was a very good flat, the rent exorbitant, but it was central in the over-crowded city, and Lilli had been delighted to find it.

Carmen watched as Quincy rang the door bell. As the door jerked open Lilli flew through it, laughing. 'Quincy, I don't believe it, I really don't . . .' She stopped, seeing that her sister wasn't alone, and Quincy said politely: 'This is Carmen Lister, the editor of *Vibes*, the magazine who ran the competition—Carmen, this is my sister, Lilli.'

'Hi,' said Carmen, running narrowed and very sharp eyes over Lilli, her face reflecting the surprise of seeing someone so beautiful.

Lilli smiled back. 'Hello—come in, both of you.'

She was so supple you almost felt she was entirely boneless, her slender body light in movement, graceful as an autumn leaf floating down from a tree. Her awareness of her body was constant, she did everything as perfectly as it was possible to do it, her gestures and smiles elegant and delicate, with the sort of effortless perfection achieved only by years of hard training disguised deliberately so that art might be mistaken for sheer accident. She was wearing black jeans and a formal white shirt, ruffles of lace tumbling down the front of it. Her red hair burnt in the dusty London air as she walked across her tiny sitting-room.

It amused Quincy to see Carmen Lister's expression. The look of amused condescension had gone. Lilli was not someone to be treated with condescension.

'I'm having a hard time making myself believe Quincy has got herself a date with Joe Aldonez,' said Lilli, smiling. It wasn't an unkind smile, merely one of laughing disbelief. Quincy loved her sister, but she felt her teeth meeting as Carmen and Lilli looked at each other in comprehension.

'We're very happy with her,' Carmen said coolly. 'She's perfect for what Joe's press agent wants.'

'I can see why,' said Lilli, and laughed again. 'But I can't help thinking my little sister needs a bodyguard if she's going to be exposed to Joe Aldonez's charm. She'll be playing way out of her league. She won't have a clue how to tackle him.'

Carmen gave her a patronising smile. 'She'll cope just for one evening, it will be the memory of a life time, something to tell her grandchildren about.'

Quincy wanted to scream and bite the furniture. Who did they think they were talking about?

'We'll have a lot of work to do on her first,' Carmen added, and both girls looked at her with neutral, assessing eyes.

'You can say that again,' Lilli sighed. Her long, graceful fingers tapped on the curve of her chin, her nails polished and gleaming. 'What did you have in mind?'

The question sent a wave of chill alarm through Quincy. She did not like the way they were surveying her, like architects regarding a building they are about to tear down and mould closer to the heart's desire.

'Her hair,' said Carmen, shuddering. 'Just look at it!'

Lilli looked and made a wry face. 'And her clothes, of course,' she suggested. 'A good manicure, a facial, a few saunas and some hours in the gym . . .'

'Am I going out with a singer or training for the Olympics?' Quincy asked sarcastically, but they ignored her.

'First we have to set up a session with a photographer,' Carmen said. 'I thought we'd have some before and after shots—some pictures of her before

she has the date with Joe and another set taken afterwards.'

What was this date supposed to do for her? Quincy
wondered. Turn her into a raving beauty?

Glancing around the little room, Carmen inspected
everything in it carefully. 'Can we have a photographer
here tomorrow? Joe and the rest of his crew will be in
Liverpool for a few days, we'll have plenty of time. I'd
like some pictures of her here with you and then some
taken of her going around some London tourist traps.'

Lilli smiled, giving Carmen a nod. 'Be my guest,
can I come along when she goes around London?'

'Why not?' shrugged Carmen. 'Great idea—you're
showing her the sights, the two of you should make
some great pictures.' She walked to the door. 'I'll be
along around ten o'clock tomorrow, don't let her out
of your sight, will you? I don't want any of this story
breaking through other channels. I have this exclusive,
remember! Or the whole thing is off!'

When she had gone, Quincy collapsed into a chair,
closing her eyes with a deep sigh. The whole day had
been a strain, she was exhausted and it was wonderful
to be able to relax and feel at home.

Lilli stood in front of her in a classic dancer's pose,
her hands on her slender hips, her feet placed carefully,
one heel tucked neatly into the instep of the other foot.

'I couldn't believe my eyes when I saw those pictures
of you in the paper. I thought I was hallucinating.'

'You and me both,' Quincy agreed without opening
her eyes. It helped to tell herself it wasn't really happening—it might be the response of the ostrich, digging its head into the sand, but it certainly made her
feel more able to go through with this whole ridiculous
charade. If she kept telling herself she had fallen down

a rabbit hole and was in a crazy Wonderland where nothing was real, she could cope with things.

'You aren't very talkative,' Lilli remarked. 'What's he really like? Come on, Quincy, give! Tell me all about him, I'm dying to hear some of the inside story.'

'Don't ask me,' said Quincy. 'Ask his publicity department, they invented him.' Her voice held an unaccountable sting which surprised her as much as her sister and she opened her eyes a second later, angry with herself.

Lilli was staring at her, round-eyed. 'Well, well,' she drawled, starting to smile. 'That doesn't sound like an adoring fan.'

'I'm not,' Quincy said furiously, getting up. 'I didn't even fill in that stupid competition form—Bobby did. Didn't Mum tell you what happened?'

'No,' said Lilli, looking even more surprised.

Quincy told her and Lilli laughed a good deal, which at first annoyed Quincy, and then made her suddenly start to laugh too, seeing the funny side of it for the first time.

'What a hoot!' grinned Lilli. 'Trust Bobby—that boy is a hatful of surprises!' Her face softened as she said that—there was a strong bond of affection between Lilli and Bobby. The long gap between them, in age, had made their relationship a very special one. By the time Bobby was born, Lilli had been a skinny, long-legged schoolgirl already obsessed with dancing, spending all her spare time limbering up and doing ballet exercises, but she had been fascinated by the new baby and eager to take care of him when she was at home. She had spent little time with him since she went away to London, but that old fondness still persisted. Between Lilli and Quincy there had always been a trace of rivalry. They were so close in age, both girls, and they had competed instinctively, quarrelled over possessions, argued and squabbled. That rivalry had died down as they grew up, especially after Lilli left home, but they had never been as close as Lilli and Bobby had been.

'You spoilt him,' Quincy accused, half laughing.

'Of course I didn't,' denied Lilli. 'Boys will be boys, that's all.'

'And Joe Aldonez was probably spoilt by his mother,' Quincy went on, ignoring that. 'He was certainly spoilt by someone. He goes around the world expecting women to fall at his feet.'

'How fascinating,' said Lilli, amused. 'And did you?'

'No, I didn't!' Quincy snapped, bright pink.

'Why are you crimson, then?' Lilli asked.

'Because I'm annoyed,' Quincy threw back.

'If you say so.' Lilli began to whistle softly, her lips pursed, and Quincy glared at her. 'What shall we do about supper?' Lilli went on to ask. 'I'm not a great cook. There's some salad in the fridge, or we could go out to the local Chinese restaurant.'

They went out, in the end, and had spare ribs and chicken in lemon sauce, with fortune cookies served with their tea afterwards. Lilli refused them, but Quincy ate one and spread out the little fortune on the table to read it. Irritably she crumpled it up and threw it in the ash tray.

'What did it say?' Lilli asked.

'Nothing,' said Quincy.

Lilli quickly fished it out and read it, giving Quincy a wicked grin. 'When the hunter spreads his nets, the wise bird stays in the air,' she read aloud. 'Sound advice, Quincy,' she teased. 'I hope you remember it.'

Quincy looked around for the waiter. 'Shall we go?' she asked. 'I'll pay the bill—this is my treat. Thanks for having me to stay, I'll try not to get in your way too much in the flat.'

She shared her sister's bedroom, sleeping on a small and very uncomfortable fold-away bed which, when not in use, doubled as a table. Quincy found it hard to get to sleep because she kept expecting the contraption to fold up with her inside it.

Carmen Lister and a photographer arrived as arranged next day and Quincy gloomily allowed herself to be posed around the flat, and then, for the rest of the day, to be shepherded around London and photographed looking at the Tower of London or the Old Bailey, feeling very silly and conscious of a build-up of impatience and resentment inside herself. She felt like a wooden doll whose arms and legs were manipulated by someone else. Her smile creaked and her head ached. It was all so crazy, so pointless. Why was she doing it? There must be an easier way of getting Bobby a transistor, she told herself, and shied away from admitting inwardly that her desire to acquire a good new radio for her brother was not the only motive for her being here. She had agreed to co-operate largely because she had been hypnotised by Joe Aldonez into doing so.

She went to bed early that evening. Next morning Carmen arrived alone and took her off to a beauty parlour in Mayfair. Quincy felt very conspicuous as she walked through the scented, busy atmosphere. Women in expensive clothes stared after her, raising eyebrows. She was not the sort of client a place like that usually had—her clothes immediately stamped her as someone without money, and her pink cheeks made her embarrassment and uneasiness obvious.

Carmen sat her in a chair and then she and a young man in an immaculate blue nylon tunic which gave him the air of being a society doctor paying a house call walked around Quincy and studied her clinically from all angles. Quincy's nervous eyes followed them. What were they planning to do to her? she wondered, wishing she was back at home.

'Beautiful hair,' the young man said. 'But it looks as if it's never seen a professional hairdresser—no style at all.' He took a comb out of his tunic pocket and flipped it through the thick chestnut curls, letting them fall back a second later. 'Most of it must go,' he said, and Quincy gave a stifled squawk of protest.

'Darling, it's far too thick, you must spend half your life combing out tangles,' he told her kindly. 'Your face has a lovely bone structure—let's see it. I'll give you a cut which will alter the whole shape of your face and let the real you shine through.'

Who is the real me? Quincy wondered, staring at her own reflection in the mirror opposite. And how would he know, anyway?

She spent most of the day in the beauty parlour, becoming increasingly cross. Carmen returned her to the flat around four o'clock and when Lilli opened the door to her she stared in total disbelief at the new Quincy.

'You look marvellous,' she said as Quincy stamped past.

'I feel like taking up residence in a cupboard,' Quincy muttered. She sank into an armchair and Lilli inspected her light, cropped curls, her expertly made-up face, her carefully manicured nails.

'What's wrong?' Lilli asked, looking puzzled. 'Darling, you do really look terrific.'

'I don't know,' muttered Quincy, not meeting her eyes.

'You're tired,' Lilli said.

'I suppose so—I think I'll go to bed early again, London is exhausting.'

Lilli stared shrewdly at her. 'What you need is some time to yourself,' she said, and Quincy groaned.

'Do I not! I'm so sick of being dragooned around London by Carmen Lister. I don't even like her, she's a very bossy lady, she never asks me what I think, she tells me.'

Lilli laughed. 'I should think that's why she's at the top of her profession. *Vibes* has a very big circulation. When is she coming to take you to buy those clothes?'

'Tomorrow afternoon. She said she would arrive around two-thirty and I was to be waiting.' Quincy's green eyes flashed. 'She orders me around as if I was a six-year-old!'

The doorbell went and Lilli made a face. 'Now who can that be?' Quincy relaxed in the chair as her sister left the room. If only she could be alone for a few days, walking through the spring fields at home, listening to the larks singing high above the dewy pastures, breathing the fresh crisp morning air and feeling free, without all the pressures which this trip to London had brought to bear. London itself seemed part of the pressure—the great, sprawling city held so many people, millions of strangers busily occupied with their own lives, indifferent to everyone else and always rushing past without being aware of anything but their own affairs. Back home she knew everyone who lived in the little village, walking down the one street she got smiles from all who passed, she knew their homes, their children, even their pets. She was a deeply embedded part of that world—here she found it hard to believe she existed at all, except as a doll which Carmen Lister was manipulating for her own purposes.

Lilli came back into the room with a large, power-fully built man in an expensive dark overcoat who glanced at Quincy briefly before looking at her sister again in query.

Lilli introduced them, smiling. 'Quincy, this is Mark Latimer, who produces our show—Mark, my sister Quincy. I told you about her and Joe Aldonez, didn't I?'

Mark Latimer offered his hand, nodding. 'I'd read about it,' he said. 'How does it feel to be suddenly famous?' He had a wry, deep voice with a resonant timbre which matched his build. Quincy got the feeling he was not a man to argue with—although his smile was pleasant it was clear from the strength of his features that he liked his own way, was accustomed to being obeyed. That air of authority sat comfortably on him, he had presence; even Lilli visibly kept her distance, treating him with respect.

'She isn't sure she likes it,' said Lilli, answering for her.

Quincy felt Mark Latimer's grey eyes assessing her. 'You must bring her over to the studio while she's in town,' was all he said. 'Perhaps she would like to watch rehearsals for an hour.' Quincy was left with the strong impression that he was conferring a great honour on her by the suggestion, but, having unbent so far, he

turned to Lilli and went on without a pause: 'I'm calling a rehearsal tomorrow at nine-thirty—that new rou-
tine just isn't smooth enough. It needs a lot of work.
Sue must take you through it until you've got it together.'

'Okay,' Lilli said meekly.

'And I've asked Wardrobe to come up with something better than those feathered costumes—you look
like a flock of pink ducks in them.' His tone was
scathing, his brows heavy with impatience. From the
streaks of silver running through his dark hair, Quincy
imagined he was a man in his forties and the air of
command made it clear that he was a very important
man, expecting exactly the sort of instant obedience he
was getting from Lilli. He was far from good-looking—
his face too heavy for that, the leonine head breathing
force rather than charm, power rather than kindness.
He talked and Lilli nodded.

He turned to Quincy a few moments later, gave her
another distant smile. 'Perhaps we'll meet again while
you're in town,' he said, and walked to the door with
Lilli at his heels, escorting him, her slender figure
entirely dwarfed by him.

When she came back, she looked eagerly at Quincy:
'What do you think of Mark?'

'A bit alarming, isn't he?' Quincy commented, and
her sister looked faintly indignant.

'He's a real powerhouse, just being with him makes
me feel twice as alive, he gets the last ounce out of
everyone who works with him.'

'Yes, I can imagine that,' said Quincy, not sure she
would enjoy close contact with a man like that. Mark
Latimer had an electric charge which Quincy suspected
would keep you on your toes all day but which would

drain you of energy very rapidly.

'He's marvellous,' Lilli said dreamily, and her sister gave her a surprised, probing stare. It was not like Lilli to be so reverential, so deeply impressed by anyone, but then Lilli had always admired people stronger than herself. She spent all her time in the pursuit of excellence, determined to be better than anyone else, and she understood a man like Mark Latimer, who obviously shared her attitudes.

Quincy spent the following morning alone, to her relief. Lilli was rehearsing and Quincy had the little flat to herself. When she was bored with the silence of the flat she went out for a walk along the river, staring at the buildings on the opposite bank, watching the sun glance off the grey water, watching the red London buses grinding their way through thick traffic. She found herself at the Tate Gallery and on impulse went in and wandered around idly with no real idea what she wanted to see. The cloistered atmosphere of the gallery suited her mood. She felt like a rabbit in a burrow, hiding from the threat of the surface world. When she emerged she took with her no lasting memory of the modern art she had walked past, but she felt more relaxed, much calmer and able to face Carmen Lister later that day.

Carmen whisked her off to buy clothes at the boutique of a London fashion house—they were ready-made clothes, but Quincy was a standard size and easy to fit. Carmen chose what she was to wear and, since she was paying, Quincy let her do so. She no longer felt it mattered. Carmen and her friends were turning Quincy into someone else. The minute she got home, Quincy had decided, she would throw off these unreal, unrecognisable pretences and return to normal, retrieve herself and forget this trip to London and all the maddening circumstances of it.

'Did you see Joe on TV last night?' Carmen asked her as she drove her back to Lilli's flat.

'No,' said Quincy, starting. 'Why was he on TV?'

'There was an item on a news programme about him—the Liverpool concert was a sell-out and a huge success, he got mobbed by the fans.' Carmen smiled. 'But then he always does—if he didn't have some pretty heavy security they'd eat him alive!'

Quincy winced. She said nothing, but when she was alone she wondered how Joe could stand that sort of contant pressure. She was to see his fans in action that evening. Watching TV, her whole system jerked alive when she suddenly found herself staring at Joe. The piece was largely concerned with his second concert, showing him singing a Spanish love song. Joe was all in black—tight-fitting satinised pants, a figure-moulding silk shirt, black leather boots—and during the song he held a red rose between his brown fingers. As he took the applause he flung it into the audience and a scramble started. Girls screamed, fought, wept. The rose was torn to shreds, a drift of scarlet petals showering the front rows. Quincy was staring at Joe. He went on smiling, but his smile was stiff, his dark eyes concerned. Hurriedly he gestured to his group, who began to play again, and he broke into another song. It had the effect he wished—the screaming fans sank back into their seats, hypnotised by the sensual throbbing voice, as if the animal hysteria which had been released in them was being lulled back to sleep by Joe's music.

Quincy got up and switched off the set as the programme passed on to other topics. She sat staring at nothing for a long time—that glimpse of Joe's world oppressed her for hours.

Having worked whatever magic she felt she could, Carmen left Quincy more or less alone over the next couple of days. They expected Joe back in London on the following Thursday—his big concert was on the Friday evening and his dinner date with Quincy would be on the Saturday.

'That's your big day,' Carmen told her. 'We have it all worked out. All you have to do is look as good as you can and leave the rest to us.' She gave Quincy a patronising nod. 'And don't worry, nobody expects you to be anything but yourself.'

'How reassuring,' said Quincy with slight tartness.

Lilli was feeling rather guilty because she was too busy to spend much time with her sister. Mark Latimer kept her busy all day rehearsing for their new series—shooting was to start the following week and he was not satisfied with their routines, Lilli confided.

'Nothing but the best for Mark,' she said with apparent satisfaction. 'He won't take second-best.' A grin flashed over her face as she added: 'If you were dying and Mark didn't think you'd done the death scene well enough he'd call you back from the tomb for a repeat performance.'

'What a lovely man,' Quincy said sarcastically, and Lilli laughed.

'He's better than any producer I ever worked with—he makes you feel so good when you've hit what he wants that all the work he's forced you to put into it seems more than worthwhile.'

The evening before Joe was due back, Quincy and Lilli were supposed to be going out to dinner, but at seven Lilli had still not arrived home from the studios.

She rang, breathless, heaving and apologetic, to say she might not get there until nine.

'Why don't you make your way to the restaurant and I'll join you as soon as I can?' she asked.

'I'd rather skip it altogether, if you don't mind,' Quincy told her. 'I'm not really in a mood to sit through a prolonged meal.'

'Oh, Quincy! I've spoiled your evening, I'm sorry!'

'Don't be silly, I wasn't very excited about it anyway, I'm rather tired. London makes me feel half dead,' Quincy sighed.

'Look, are you sure . . .' started Lilli, and Quincy assured her firmly that she was certain.

'I'd just love to go to bed with a book and relax,' she confessed. 'Sorry to be a bore, but I'm not used to all this high living. After spending all day exploring London on buses all I want to do is flop like a rag doll.'

Lilli laughed. 'I remember the feeling—I felt like that when I first got here, London is pretty exhausting when you're not used to it. Look, Quincy, I must rush, Mark's shouting for me.'

'Don't keep the big man waiting,' Quincy said drily. ' 'Bye!'

She put the phone down. Everyone here seemed to be in such a rush, so busy getting somewhere that they never had time to notice anything along the way. Quincy trailed into the bathroom and ran a warm bath, soaked herself for half an hour in perfumed foamy water, letting her body and her tired mind collapse into complete inactivity. She was homesick, she wanted to be back with her parents and Bobby, where she belonged. London was a madhouse.

She climbed out, dripping, towelled herself and

slipped into a short white robe, tying it firmly around her waist. Her hair curled damply in soft clusters around her pink face as, barefoot, she walked through to the bedroom. Pulling back the covers, she was about to climb into the bed when the doorbell rang. A frown creased her brows. Had Lilli got back from the studio earlier than she had expected?

She went to the door and opened it, a smile ready, only to find herself facing Joe. He was leaning on the doorframe in a weary attitude, his long lean body languidly disposed as though he could hardly stay on his feet. His face was almost haggard, his tan only just disguising the exhaustion, his cheekbones locked in a mask of taut compression.

The dark eyes stared at her almost blankly. 'Can I come in?' he asked huskily. Quincy put a trembling hand to her robe lapels, pulling them closer.

'I was just going to bed,' she said. 'I'm sorry, but . . .'

'I need to talk to you,' Joe said abruptly with harsh force.

Quincy's breath caught, her eyes fixed on him. Without a word she fell back and Joe walked past her into the flat.

CHAPTER FOUR

HE walked into the sitting-room and Quincy followed, switching on the lamp. The room glowed warmly and Joe stood, hunched in his heavy sheepskin jacket, his black hair windswept, looking around him half dazedly, as though uncertain where he was.

'I thought you were flying back to London tomorrow,' said Quincy, and he gave a curt nod.

'We were supposed to—there was a big reception for us tonight in Bristol, but I couldn't face it. I had to get away, I was dead.'

He looked dead, every line of his face and body stamped with a weariness she had never expected to see in him.

'Would you like a drink?' she asked. 'Have you eaten?'

He looked vaguely at her. 'Eaten?' From his voice the idea of food had never entered his mind. 'No, I don't think so,' he added.

'I'll get you something, what would you like?'

He shrugged indifferently. 'Whatever you have on hand, I'm easy.'

Quincy went over to the electric fire and switched it on to give the room more warmth—there was central heating in the flat, but it gave a background warmth which was not quite sufficient on a chill spring night.

Joe was still standing in the middle of the room, his hands hanging at his sides. She turned and looked at him uncertainly. 'Sit down, the room should warm up soon.'

He sat obediently, like a child, and then collapsed, his head back against the couch, his eyes closing. Quincy stared at him, frowning. His lids were dark and shadowed, bruised with tiredness, beneath his eyes the blue stain of sleepless nights emphasising the taut stretch of his skin.

'I had to come,' he said in a hazy voice which drifted from his barely parted lips like mist.

She almost wondered if she had imagined it, so faint

was the remark, and waited a moment for him to add
something, but he seemed asleep, his long body heavily
relaxed. Slowly she went out to the tiny kitchen
adjoining the room and looked at the assembled food.
There was rice and some cold chicken, a tiny tin of
prawns, some eggs. Quincy hesitated, then got out a
saucepan and began to cook a reduced version of paella.
While it was cooking she slipped back to look at Joe.
He hadn't moved, his breathing deep and slow. Was
he asleep? she wondered, and tiptoed out again, but,
as she did, he stirred and his eyes opened.

Quincy halted, looking into them, and Joe smiled at
her, a curiously tender, almost relieved smile.

'I was taking a nap,' he said. 'Having a dream. I
dreamt I was here with you. God, Quincy, I'm so
tired.'

'Yes,' she said gently. 'Are you hungry? I'm cooking
some paella for you. Do you like paella?'

Humour sparked in his eyes. 'You ask me that? If
my mother could hear you!' His voice was still flat and
tired, but warmth and rest were just beginning to ease
the constriction of his face.

'I'm afraid it won't be anything like any paella you
ever ate,' Quincy said, smiling. 'I'm having to im-
provise.'

'I shan't be over-critical,' he promised, and she went
out to see how the food was coming along. By the time
she was ready to serve it Joe had been there for nearly
half an hour. She went back and found he had shed his
sheepskin and was stretched out, the electric fire close
to his feet, staring intently at the glowing bars. He
looked up as she entered the room and smiled.

'Feeling better?' she asked, seeing that he looked
far more relaxed, and he nodded. 'Your paella is

ready,' Quincy told him.

'Are you having some?' he asked. 'I don't want to eat alone.'

So they ate the food together with a bottle of Lilli's cheap red wine to accompany it. Joe talked in fits and starts, saying whatever came into his mind. Quincy said very little, but she listened.

'It gets to the stage when I haven't any more to give,' said Joe. 'You keep giving out night after night until your head feels as if it's blowing off and you have to get away.'

Quincy refilled his glass and he drank some more wine, eyes half closed. 'You only have so much energy,' he said.

He told her obliquely about the tour, leaving her with the impression that he barely knew what he was saying. His mind was wandering, awash with confused memories he had not yet sorted out into any sort of sense. 'They grab at you from all sides, hands dragging at you. I sometimes wonder what it is they want, what they're hoping you'll give them. If it went on too long you'd get frightened—so much need, so much emotion, and there isn't enough in any one person to satisfy them.'

He had stopped eating and she began to collect up the plates. 'Leave them,' said Joe, frowning like a fretful child. Quincy sat down again and asked: 'Coffee?'

'Yes,' he said, and got up, too, and went back to the couch. She watched him stretch out, then softly cleared the little table and went to make the coffee. He had his eyes shut again when she came back with the tray. She would have quietly crept out once more if he hadn't opened his eyes and looked at her again.

That smile was back. 'I always feel you there,' he

said. 'Isn't that odd? You're so quiet, but I can feel you if you're in the same room.' He shut his eyes again in that abrupt way and Quincy put down the tray and sat on the couch to pour the coffee. She had the feeling Joe was still not quite aware of what he was saying or doing. His mind was totally blown, he was in a state of nervous collapse after the tension of the concerts.

Turning to see if he was awake enough to drink his coffee, she found him watching her with half-raised lids, the gleaming jet of his eyes showing through his lashes.

He lazily put out a hand and pulled her down towards him. Quincy let herself curl against his body, her mouth dry as Joe tipped up her chin and began to kiss her softly.

She did not feel she was in any danger from Joe tonight—he was far too tired. That was why he was here, why he had come to her—he was in desperate need of a female presence which would comfort, not demand, which would give, not take.

Her lips parted, a curious trembling beginning deep inside her, her hand lifting to his windswept black hair, stroking it back from his face, her fingers combing through it and shaping the modelling of his skull beneath. Joe murmured huskily, his hand at her waist, and slid sideways, drawing her with him so that they lay on the couch entwined, their bodies warm and close. His kiss deepened without force, the movements of his mouth hungry, as though her warmth flowed into him and renewed him, her life force recharging his.

Her arm around his neck, her thighs tangled with his, she felt his heart beating slowly and heavily against her own, but there was still no threat in their embrace.

Even while he kissed her and his hand moved softly over her he seemed on the verge of sleep, the gentle movements of their mouths soothing him, his body entirely relaxed.

She was so much at ease that her body jerked with shock as Joe's fingers moved inside her robe to find the warm, naked flesh beneath.

'No!' she broke out with a gasp, but his mouth silenced the little cry, gently caressing her lips to prevent them from denying him that access to her. She put a hand up to his shoulder to thrust him away, and he caught it and twined his fingers with hers, clasping her hand against his softly breathing chest.

Quincy felt the languid exploration of his other hand with an explosive awareness, her nerves on fire throughout her whole body, her nipples hardening as his fingertips brushed over them, her white flesh swelling as his palm cupped it and made her skin ache with the heated blood beneath.

He would not release her mouth, coaxing her lips, playing with them, his tongue tip flicking softly and making her tremble, faint moans of pleasure breathed into his mouth. She had forgotten everything but the intense sensuality of his lovemaking, led blindfold, step by step, into a trap she had not suspected, her caution abandoned in what she imagined to be his extreme exhaustion. He had deftly undone his own shirt while he held her hand against him, and laid her fingers on his warm, bare chest before curving his free hand around the back of her head, his fingers gripping her hair, holding her captive while he kissed her with a growing passion.

'I need you,' he breathed huskily, and a pulse beat like a cruel drum deep inside her, the aroused ache of desire taking her over and holding her helpless in his arms.

'I can't,' she whispered, trying to break free, raising herself desperately.

'Quincy,' he muttered, his eyes open now, staring up at her flushed, disturbed face.

'Don't!' She hardly knew what she was begging him not to do—he was using no force now, he was only gazing at her with dark eyes filled with a need echoed inside herself, his whole face taut with the same desire which was throbbing inside her.

He had undone her belt and the white towelling robe had fallen open, leaving her naked body visible. Joe's gaze travelled slowly, hungrily, over the smooth curve of it from breast to waist, from slim rounded hips to the pale thighs, and Quincy's face burned under the impact of that desiring stare, feeling his eyes imprinted on her naked skin like fiery branding marks.

'If you wanted a woman, why didn't you take one of those who throw themselves at you?' she burst out hoarsely. 'I'm not on offer!'

She scrambled up and Joe made no attempt to detain her, letting her go, his hand limply falling back.

She turned and stood with her back to him. 'You'd better go,' she muttered.

She heard the slow, stiff movement as he forced himself to get up. He did not go, however. He stood there, giving a heavy sigh.

'I'm sorry, Quincy. I had no right . . .'

'No, you hadn't!' she interrupted angrily.

'I didn't come here with that in mind,' he said wearily. 'That wasn't my intention. I just didn't think at all. I needed some safe place to be, some comfort. I miss my family when I'm on tour. I was driven by instinct, I was acting blind. I'm sorry.'

She was silent, then, her belt tied tightly again, her head bent, the light soft curls tumbled forward, leaving her nape bare.

'What have you done to your beautiful hair?' Joe asked, as if he had just noticed the change in her appearance. 'Why have you cut it off? It was lovely just the way it was.'

'Carmen took me to a beauty parlour,' Quincy started, and heard him swear softly.

'Why did you let her change you?' he almost accused.

'It seemed to be part of the deal,' Quincy explained. 'You're all set on your own way, you never ask, just try to make everyone give in to you.'

He gave a wrenched, angry sigh. 'I'm sorry.'

'Stop saying that, you don't mean it!'

'Why would I say it if I didn't?' he asked in that low, weary voice. She felt him right behind her and before she could stiffen and move away he had brushed his lips lightly over her exposed nape. 'I am sorry, Quincy, believe it or not as you choose,' he said, then walked away towards the door.

Quincy watched the slow tired movements of his body. He had his sheepskin jacket over his arm and she sensed that his muscles were only just obeying him. Now that the fevered need inside him had stopped driving him, he was back in his state of blind exhaustion.

'You'd better stay the night,' she said almost crossly, and he stopped and looked round at her, surprise in his face.

'You can sleep on the couch,' she said. 'I'll get you some blankets.'

'Sure?' Joe asked, but he was already retracing his steps.

'Yes, I'll catch Lilli before she comes in here—you'll be able to sleep undisturbed.'

He sank down on the couch, lying full length, his eyes closing, the lashes sinking on to his strong brown cheeks. By the time Quincy got back with two spare blankets, he was asleep, his head turned sideways against a cushion, his arm flung up to guard his eyes from the light. Quincy stood looking down at him, a queer little pain inside her chest, a jab of tenderness for him that hurt. Gently she covered him with the blankets and he stirred briefly, mumbling, without opening his eyes.

She walked to the door and switched off the light, then went out, shutting the door behind her. She was going into the bedroom when Lilli let herself in at the front door and halted, surprise in her face.

'Still up? I expected you to be in bed by now. Quin, I'm sorry about tonight, honestly. Rehearsals just went on and on, I thought I'd never get away. Mark wouldn't give up until he had something approaching what he wanted.'

'It doesn't matter,' Quincy assured her, and, as her sister went to walk past, stepped into her path, shaking her head. 'Don't go into the sitting-room, Joe Aldonez is asleep on our couch.'

Lilli stared at her with disbelief, her eyes rounding. 'What did you say?'

'Joe Aldonez is asleep on our couch,' said Quincy, knowing she had flushed.

'That was what I thought you said,' Lilli told her, taking her arm and pulling her into the bedroom. She shut the door and turned to stare at Quincy. 'Am I going to get an explanation, or do I just guess?' she asked, and there was something strange in her face.

Quincy stared, baffled, for a second, then hot colour rushed up her face. 'You don't think ... well ... Lilli!'

'Coherent, aren't you?' said Lilli, starting to laugh and relaxing a little at the stammered words. 'So you and Mr Aldonez haven't been making whoopee on my couch?'

'No!' Quincy snapped angrily, refusing to remember the hectic lovemaking which had begun and would probably have gone on until now if she hadn't pulled herself together.

'Then what's he doing here?'

'He was so tired,' Quincy explained. 'His tour was exhausting and he walked out on the final party. I think he came here because they wouldn't think of looking for him here ...'

'They?' asked Lilli, looking puzzled.

Quincy shrugged. 'The people who run his life— men like Billy Griffith, his manager. From what Joe said to me he rarely has any time to himself, he works far too hard. Suddenly he was sick of it all, and he bolted.'

Lilli studied her curiously. 'To you,' she said in a very soft, thoughtful voice.

'What?' Quincy tried to look blank and baffled, but her lips curved in a little smile. Joe had come to find her and she couldn't help feeling a stab of pleasure in the thought.

Her sister was watching her. 'What's going on between you two?' she asked. 'Joe Aldonez is a top star, he must be worth millions. Why should he come to you to find a bolthole? I thought you barely knew him, have you been holding out on me, Quincy?'

'Of course not!' denied Quincy, but her eyes did not quite meet her sister's.

'Life's full of surprises,' Lilli murmured. 'I thought I knew you right through to your backbone, but it just shows—you should never take anyone at face value.'

'I don't know what you're talking about,' Quincy said crossly. 'Have you eaten, or would you like me to get you some supper?'

'Mark took us out,' said Lilli, her face changing. 'He bought us a late supper at a fish restaurant near the river.' Laughter filled her eyes. 'He was brave enough to have lobster—I hope he doesn't have trouble getting to sleep.'

'What did you have?' Quincy asked.

'I played safe and had cold salmon with salad,' Lilli told her. 'I need my beauty sleep.' She yawned, her face tired. 'Which reminds me, I must get to bed, I'm whacked.'

When they were both in bed with the light out, Quincy lay awake listening to her sister's quiet breathing, wondering how she was going to face Joe in the morning. How would he look at her, remembering tonight?

She slept so deeply that it wasn't until Lilli shook her hard that her eyes fluttered open and, dazedly, she stared up at her sister.

'Hallo, sleeping beauty, for a minute I thought I was going to have to drop a bomb to wake you up—I've been trying to get through to you for about five minutes.' Lilli gestured to a cup of tea on the bedside table. 'I made some tea. Now I've got to rush—we've got an early call for rehearsals this morning.'

Quincy sat up, yawning, for a few seconds forgetting

all that had happened last night. As she reached for the cup, memory returned in a violent flood and she halted, her lips parted on a gasp. 'Joe!' she muttered, and her sister gave her a quizzical look.

'He'd gone when I got up,' she said. 'A very polite guest, I may say—he'd folded his blankets and left the room spotlessly tidy. When you see him, tell him he's welcome to use my couch any time he needs it.'

Quincy slackened, a faint painful disappointment in her veins as she forced a smile. 'Oh, I see,' she said. He might have stayed long enough to say goodbye, she thought.

Lilli threw her another quick, amused glance, then said very softly: 'He left this for you.' Walking to the door, she tossed an envelope on to the bed. ' 'Bye, darling,' she said, as she went out, and Quincy heard her laughing to herself.

The envelope lay on the end of the bed. Quincy looked at it, trembling, then scrambled down the bed to get it and climbed back inside the sheets, sitting up with the envelope in her hand, staring at her own name written on the front of it, in a strong, bold hand.

Joe's handwriting conjured him up in front of her, the flowing lines of it black and powerful, full of certainty and assurance.

She tore it open and read the few words scribbled on to a sheet of writing paper inside. 'Thank you for last night.'

A warm blush crawled up her face from her neck. Anyone reading that might get a very false impression from the words. She was glad he had sealed it down— Lilli would certainly have misunderstood.

She drank her tea and got up, took a quick bath and got dressed in a pair of white jeans, slipping a thin

blue woollen sweater over the top of her head. Inside
the folds she didn't, at first, hear the doorbell, but as
she pulled the sweater down the insistent noise startled
her and she ran to open the door.

'Hallo, Quincy.'

She couldn't believe her eyes for a long moment,
staring at Brendan in astonishment, then she
demanded: 'What are *you* doing here?'

'I decided to take a few days off,' he said, but he was
rather uneasy, his face betraying uncertainty. 'Can I
come in?' he asked, and Quincy automatically stepped
back to let him walk past her.

She followed him into the sitting-room and watched
him glancing around. He looked different in London.
At home he normally wore shabby, untidy working
clothes—tweed jackets and old sweaters, grey cords
and heavy boots. Today he was wearing a suit, and she
rarely remembered seeing Brendan in a suit. It was far
from being elegant or expensive—the dark material had
been carefully pressed, though, and his blue-striped
shirt looked new.

Suspiciously, Quincy asked: 'Now tell me the
truth—why have you come?'

Brendan was not used to evading the truth. He
couldn't meet her eyes. 'Why shouldn't I come to
London once in a blue moon?'

'It seems a strange coincidence,' Quincy accused.
'Did my parents suggest you came?'

'Good lord, no!' Brendan denied, and this time he
did look at her, his face surprised. 'They don't even
know,' he added, and she believed him.

Quincy hesitated, frowning. She was very fond of
Brendan, but she prickled with resentment at the idea
that he had followed her to London in order to keep

an eye on her. 'If you've come with some idea of protecting me from big bad wolves, you can take the first train home, Brendan,' she said crossly. 'I'm in no danger from anyone.'

'Aren't you?' Brendan asked rather gloomily. 'I suspect you wouldn't even know if you were—you're not used to dealing with men like Aldonez, Quincy, he's far too sophisticated for you, and he'd be ruthless to get his own way.'

A flicker of doubt showed in her face. She was about to deny what Brendan had said, angrily throw it back at him, but then she remembered the smooth way Joe had gradually seduced her into those meltingly sweet kisses, his approach so slow and gentle she had felt quite safe with him until she realised how far they had gone.

'I'm quite capable of dealing with him!' she said, stiffening. 'I'm only here for another couple of days, I can assure you I'm coping with things perfectly well.'

Brendan grimaced wryly. 'That sounds to me like a prepared speech,' he told her.

'Don't be silly!'

'You sound like someone whistling in the dark,' Brendan added. 'Your father's worried about you.'

'Dad?' She searched his face anxiously. 'Did he say so?'

'Every time you ring he looks worried,' Brendan told her. 'He hasn't needed to tell me anything. I can read his face.'

Quincy walked to the window and stared down into the busy street below. 'Maybe he picked up that I was feeling rather fed up,' she said. 'The magazine editor has been hustling me around London like a sheepdog with a stray sheep and I was sick of it.'

'You've done something to your hair,' Brendan noticed. 'I like it,' he added. 'It's very pretty like that.'

'Thank you,' said Quincy, turning to smile at him. It was very kind of him to come all this way with an idea of protecting her, even if it was galling that he should feel she needed protection.

His face brightened as he saw that her first flare of irritation had faded. 'I suppose you wouldn't come out and show me London?' he asked. 'We could have lunch somewhere.'

She hesitated, her eyes on the couch behind him, then her face hardened. Last night she had come very close to giving Joe Aldonez what he wanted and she was not so innocent that she didn't realise he might have been playing with her, deliberately exaggerating his own weariness in order to seduce her. Quincy looked ahead to the next few days, alarmed. Joe had somehow gained an advantage over her last night. In the dangerous duel between them he had snatched several points from her without her understanding what was happening. He might well plan to wage a campaign from now on which, he could hope, would end in Quincy weakly surrendering. Maybe Brendan was right. Maybe Joe was ruthless. How could she be certain either way? She barely knew him; she knew Brendan. Only a blind fool would trust a man whose background was so different from her own.

Brendan saw the uncertainty in her eyes. 'Please, Quincy,' he pressed, and she nodded.

'Okay, I'll get ready—where did you want to go?'

'You're my guide,' he said, looking delighted. 'What should I see? The weather is so terrific I thought we could go for a trip on the river.'

'I haven't done that yet,' Quincy said. 'I'd love it—

you get the boat from Charing Cross Pier on the
embankment. You can go up river towards Windsor, or
down towards the sea. Whichever way you go, you get a
great view of London.'

When they left the flat, she saw that Brendan had
not been exaggerating—the morning had that clear,
bright freshness which spring sometimes gives to surprise you, the sky cloudless blue, the wind brisk but
not sharp, and the trees along the Embankment bursting out into full leaf, it seemed, overnight.

'Why don't we walk to Charing Cross?' Brendan
suggested, so they walked quickly along the river,
following the twists and turns of it as it lay chained
within the old concrete walls rising from the river
bank. On the far side of the water, the windows of
office blocks flashed back the sunlight at them, and
a motorboat chugged past, dipping and rising on the
choppy waves.

'What have you been up to while you've been here?'
Brendan asked, and she told him with wry self-
mockery.

'I felt a fool,' she ended, and Brendan looked at her,
nodding.

'I'm not surprised. They're using you.'

'I'm not that much of a fool,' Quincy snapped. 'I
realised that. I'm angry with myself for agreeing to
come here in the first place, but I let myself be talked
into it, and now it's too late to back out.' She stopped,
sighing. 'There are only another few days to go then
I'll be back home,' she ended, wishing her heart did
not sink as she said that.

They reached Charing Cross to find that the only
boat available was going down past St Paul's and
Tower Bridge and they quickly got tickets and

went on board. Although the weather was bright, the water was far from calm and trip was distinctly lively. Quincy and Brendan sat on the open deck, clinging to the rail, watching the grey waves churning along the side of the hull. The London skyline edged the river on each side, many of the landmarks so familiar that they did not need the voice of the guide on the tannoy to point them out. Quincy stared in horrified fascination at the crumbling old wharf which had once been the scene of executions during the dangerous time when pirates sailed the seas of the world. Convicted pirates had been chained to the dock to await the rising tide which would drown them, the guide told them, making her shudder.

'I went to the London Dungeon yesterday,' she told Brendan. 'The waxworks are all frightening; executions and murders, the most horrible scenes. I couldn't wait to get out.'

'Have you been to the Tower?' Brendan asked, and she nodded.

'Carmen Lister took me there.'

The boat turned back to Charing Cross half an hour later. Quincy was huddled in her coat, her skin whipped icily by the freshening wind blowing from the sea. On either bank she saw the flat, featureless marshes of Essex stretching away to a grey horizon, seabirds rising at the river edge, from the muddy shores, their spread wings flapping as they took flight.

When they reached Charing Cross again, they disembarked, walking stiffly at first before they accustomed themselves to being back on dry land. They had lunch at a popular restaurant near Trafalgar Square, traffic swirling past noisily.

'Where are you staying, Brendan?' she asked as they drank their coffee.

'A small hotel near Regent's Park,' he said. 'It's quite quiet there at night.'

Quincy glanced at her watch, frowning. 'I ought to go back to the flat in case I've been missed—Carmen Lister said she would ring me this afternoon and tell me what plans they have.'

As they left the restaurant a taxi swung past and Brendan hailed it. Quincy climbed in with more haste than common sense, and banged her head violently on the edge of the door. She sank into the seat, holding her hand to the throbbing bruise. Brendan clambered after her, told the driver where to take them, and asked Quincy anxiously if she was badly hurt.

'I'll be okay,' she said, but her head was aching so much she could not speak again for a whole minute.

It only took the taxi five minutes to cover the ground from Trafalgar Square to the flat in Chelsea and as it came to a halt outside the building Brendan got out and helped Quincy to descend, his arm around her waist. He paid the driver and looked down at her with a worried frown.

'I hope you haven't got concussion—that was quite a knock you took.'

'It's wearing off,' she said, forcing a smile.

'I'll see you into the flat,' Brendan decided firmly. 'You'd better lie down for a while—head injuries, however slight, can be dangerous.'

'Don't fuss, Brendan,' she said, then regretted speaking so sharply as he looked at her with silent reproach. 'Sorry,' she added quickly. 'Maybe you're right.'

'Does it hurt much now?'

'Not that much,' she said as they walked into the

building. She swayed very slightly as the throb from the wound began again and Brendan's arm steadied her, drawing her closer. She leaned on him, slanting a grateful smile up at him, then saw his face change as his eyes moved from her face to that of the man confronting them.

Quincy's head swung that way, too, her breath catching sharply as she took in Joe's frowning face. She had never seen that expression in it before, it startled her. He wore a savage, hostile scowl, those dark eyes icy little chips of lightless black beneath his drawn brows.

'Where the hell have you been all morning?' he ground out between straight, unsmiling lips which only just parted to let the words through.

CHAPTER FIVE

FOR a beat of time, Quincy was speechless in the face of the angry question, then she, in turn, grew angry, her eyes very bright in her flushed face as she stared back at him.

'How dare you yell at me like that? Who do you think you are? I've every right to go out if I want to, I'm not owned by anybody but myself and I'll go where I like. If you object, I'll pack my case and go home, Mr Aldonez!' The words tumbled over each other making them almost inaudible if it wasn't for the fact that she flung them at him so loudly that he couldn't help but understand them.

His features darkened even further, she heard the

savage snap of his teeth as they came together. 'Don't you scream at me, Quincy!' he snarled.

'If you can scream, so can I,' she retorted.

He took a long stride, his body pulsating with the rage she saw in his face. 'Now look here . . .'

'No,' Brendan interrupted, stepping in front of her and facing Joe, his shoulders squared, bristling with aggression. 'You look, Mr Aldonez—if you push her around you'll have me to answer to!'

Quincy heard the sudden softness of Joe's voice and a quiver of alarm ran through her. 'Oh, will I?' said Joe, almost purring, like a crouched panther just waiting for the chance to spring on an unwary victim who has wandered innocently into its path.

'Quincy isn't under any obligation to you,' Brendan informed him. 'You don't own her.'

'Do you?' Joe asked in that soft voice, and Quincy heard the hidden pulse of danger beneath the gentle tones, her skin going cold.

Brendan hesitated, but only for a second. 'If you mean, is she my girl—yes, not that it's any business of yours.'

Quincy was shaken and drew a quick breath to deny it, but Joe did not give her time to choose her words.

'I see,' he said, the syllables dragging out of him so slowly that her teeth ached with the tension of wondering what was going on inside his head. She could not see his face, Brendan stood between them, but she shifted sideways to get a glimpse of him and found him staring at Brendan dangerously, his jaw set.

As she moved, his eyes slid sideways to touch her face, and Quincy flinched at the cold contempt she saw in his gaze.

'Why did you want me?' she faltered, hating the way

he looked at her so much she felt sick.

'Carmen had set up some publicity shots,' Joe told her in a curt voice. 'I was rehearsing at the hall all morning and she thought it would be a good idea to have you there, but we couldn't track you down. Even your sister had no idea where you were.'

'She left before Brendan arrived,' Quincy mumbled. 'I hadn't expected . . .'

'I arrived without warning,' Brendan broke in, putting an arm protectively around her shoulders. 'It never occurred to either of us that anyone would worry.'

'Didn't it?' Joe demanded in that clipped, terse voice, somehow conveying that he did not believe Brendan.

'No!' Quincy assured him, faint pleading in her green eyes. 'Carmen said she'd ring me this afternoon. I thought I would be free all morning, and when Brendan arrived and suggested we go on a trip down the river I didn't think twice.'

'You're here to do publicity for us,' Joe said scathingly. 'We promised your father that we'd keep an eye on you—how do you think we felt when you vanished off the face of the earth, leaving no clue where you had gone?'

'I'm sorry, I hadn't looked at it like that,' she admitted.

'You should have left a message,' Joe flung at her. 'Going off alone without saying a word to anyone was the height of lunacy.'

'Aren't you making mountains out of molehills?' Brendan asked him impatiently.

'Who asked your opinion?' demanded Joe, turning on him, the powerful set of his shoulders declaring battle.

'I'm giving it anyway,' Brendan informed him, glaring back with a similar expression.

'Don't bother,' snapped Joe. 'Keep your opinions to yourself.'

'Talk to me like that and . . .' Brendan began, and Joe leaned towards him, smiling tightly.

'And what?' he asked.

'And you'll get a punch on the nose,' Brendan promised.

Joe smiled. 'Talk costs nothing,' he mocked, and Brendan's face went brick red.

'You . . .' He bit off the epithet and swung at Joe, but the blow never connected. Joe moved lightly and swiftly and Brendan went crashing backwards to hit the wall behind him. Quincy gave a cry of distress and anger, running towards him. The door of a flat on the floor above had opened and an old lady peered down at them from the landing, her bright eyes fascinated.

'You brute, his head's bleeding!' Quincy exclaimed as she saw Brendan reeling upright again, his hand going to the side of his skull where a little trickle of blood had begun to show.

'What did you want me to do?' Joe asked her coldly. 'Stand still and let him smash my face in?'

'What a lovely idea,' Quincy snapped back.

'Sorry, I'm not a masochist,' Joe told her.

'I know what you are!' she said. 'You're a bully—you know you're stronger than Brendan, you knew you could knock him down with one hand tied behind your back!' Her words cut off as she heard what she had said, and, aghast, she looked at Brendan, who had gone white. Quincy could have bitten her tongue out. She saw from his face that she had hurt his feelings badly, insulted him after the blow Joe had just delivered with such crushing effect.

'Thanks,' he said, stiffening.

'Brendan, I didn't . . .'

She was talking to herself. Brendan had walked out of the door and with an anxious face Quincy hurried after him, realising what a stupid, thoughtless remark that had been. It wouldn't have been quite so painful to Brendan if he had not just been forced to recognise that it was the truth.

'Where are you going?' Joe asked, catching her arm as she was at the door.

'I must speak to Brendan. How could I say such a thing? Poor Brendan, he's so upset.'

'Poor Brendan will get over it,' Joe said callously, refusing to let her go as she struggled in his iron grip.

'Will you let go?' Quincy gasped, an arm flailing towards him, pulling violently to free herself.

'No,' he said coolly. 'First things first—I have things to say to you that can't wait, you can pour sympathy out over Brendan Leary some other time.'

'Don't maul me about!' Quincy yelled, fighting in real earnest now, and half aware at the back of her mind of the silent, intrigued eye-witness on the landing above. The old lady had settled down to enjoy herself, following every word as though she was watching some film on television.

'Stand still, damn you!' Joe grated, and as Quincy dragged away from him her doorkey fell from her coat pocket, clattering to the stone floor. Still holding her, Joe bent and scooped it up. He pulled her towards the door, fighting him every step of the way while their audience on the upper floor leaned over so as to make quite sure of missing nothing of what happened. With

considerable difficulty, in the face of her struggles, Joe
managed to insert the key into the lock without releas-
ing her. The door swung open as he pushed it. Controlling
Quincy with that steel bracelet locked around her wrist,
Joe turned towards the stairs. Quincy had imagined he
was unaware of being watched, but, it seemed, he was
not—he gave a little bow and a charming smile.

'The performance is over, madam,' he said, and the
old lady straightened, going pink.

Joe manhandled Quincy, without compunction,
inside the flat and slammed the door shut behind them
with his foot. Only then did he let her go, setting his
back against the door as she darted forward, folding
his arms across his chest, a satisfied smile on his mouth
as she glared impotently at him.

'How dare you?' she seethed helplessly. 'What do
you want?'

His brows swooped upwards, mockery stealing into
his eyes, and between them flashed the memory of what
had happened in the flat the previous evening. Quincy
was even more furious at the amused reminder of her
own folly. Last night she had trusted him, been lulled
into a blind over-confidence about his intentions, but
she was not ever going to make that mistake about him
any more.

'While you're in London to do this publicity for us I
don't want you wandering off alone again,' he said
before she could burst out with a biting retort. 'We
have to know where you are every minute of the day,
and, most important of all, you must get rid of the
boy-friend.'

The insolence of that demand made her stiffen from
head to foot. 'You have no right . . .' she began, and
was interrupted.

'I've every right. It wouldn't look good in the papers if you had another guy hanging around when you were supposed to be crazy about me.'

She gave a gasp, burning with embarrassed anger. 'If that's the impression your publicity people have been giving, they can eat their words! I'm not crazy about you . . .'

'Aren't you?' he intervened smoothly, but she ignored him.

'And I won't have lies like that put into Carmen's magazine! I'm going to pack my case and go home, and you can find someone else to go through this ridiculous charade. You have thousands of fans—get one of them to do it, they'll leap at the chance.'

'Too late,' Joe drawled coolly. 'The publicity is right in full swing—haven't you been reading about yourself in the papers?'

She stared, her lips parted in surprise, and he read her expression with intent curiosity, his mouth twisting.

'Obviously not,' he said. 'Carmen has really hooked the public with her stories about you—you've caught the popular imagination. Right from that first photograph of you they were interested. Carmen's nose was right, you were a gift. It was a stroke of luck that you chose to stay with your sister, the press couldn't find you, so they had to rely on Carmen for information and she's been feeding them the sort of stuff she wanted to get into print.'

'What sort of stuff?' Quincy asked dazedly, aghast at the images he was conjuring up. What had the press been printing about her? Carmen had not breathed a word of all this, and nor had Lilli, although Lilli must have known what was going on—or had she been so involved with her rehearsals that she had missed the press stories altogether?

Joe shrugged. 'Background stories about your family and home life, about how much you love my records, how thrilled you are to actually meet me!'

Quincy turned and slowly walked into the sitting-room, sitting down before her legs gave out under her. Joe followed her and stood watching her, his long body lounging casually a foot away.

'How can you bear to let them print stories like that?' she asked bitterly, lifting her eyes to stare at him with chill hostility. 'You've made a fool of me.' In more ways than one, she reminded herself. He lived in an artificial world with a spotlight constantly surrounding him and Quincy had wandered innocently into the glare of that light, not realising at first that although her own reactions were genuine and impulsive, Joe Aldonez was never unconscious of being watched, of performing for a worldwide audience. Everything he did was a performance, Quincy thought. Outside the flat she had stupidly imagined he was unconscious of the woman watching them from the top of the stairs—she should have known better. Joe Aldonez was always aware of the eyes on him and what he did and said was never genuine.

He frowned, his brows a savage slash across his forehead, the charm absent suddenly, only the dark power visible.

'Don't be ridiculous, we've done nothing of the kind! All the coverage has been favourable, you come over as a charming girl . . .'

'It's all phoney,' Quincy flung at him, and his frown deepened. 'Like you,' she added, so angry she no longer knew exactly what she was saying, her own sense of hurt and confusion bewildering her, making her hit out wildly.

'Thank you,' he said in a deep, cold voice. 'That's what you think of me, is it?'

'Isn't that what you are? You're not real at all, you're a beautiful plastic image dreamed up by your publicity department. I bet they switch you off at night, like a Christmas tree in a shop window.'

Joe's black eyes had frozen over as he listened, the taut lines of his face locked together as though he struggled to keep his temper in the face of her angry, excited accusations.

'I'm not switched off now,' he said tersely as she stammered to a halt, hearing her own voice echoing inside her head with a sense of disbelief—had she really said such things to him? It was so out of character that she couldn't believe it had been herself talking. Even as she was biting her lower lip, Joe took a stride across the space between them and his hands closed over her shoulders, lifting her bodily from the couch.

'Let go!' Quincy yelled, and he shook her violently, looming over her and sending her heart into her mouth at the expression on his strong, dark face.

'No, Quincy, you've had your say—now you'll do some listening for a change. Do you think I enjoy all the publicity, the lack of privacy, the invasions of the fans? I put up with it because it's part of the deal. What I like to do is sing and I work hard at it—the rest of the job is a drag I could very happily do without. I have to keep reminding myself that my fans are the ones the music is for—and I try to understand why they behave the way they do, I try to give them what they're screaming for, and it isn't as simple as you may think. Life can be pretty grim for some of them these

days. How many millions are unemployed here and in
the States? If life's grey twenty-four hours a day, seven
days a week, fifty-two weeks of the year, anyone could
be excused for needing a little happiness pretty desperately. I'm very proud to think my music brings
some colour into their lives, and I never forget that
but for the grace of God I might be out there looking
for a job and not finding one. I owe the world all the
colour I can give it.'

Quincy was held immobile, like a rag doll, between
his powerful fingers, but it was not force which held
her captive, listening with widening eyes. It was the
depth in his gaze, the low hard note of his voice. Joe
wasn't acting now, his eyes sombre, his face harsh.

'I told you my mother came from Spain,' he said.
'Do you know what year she arrived in the States?
1939.'

'1939?' Quincy began, and he nodded.

'The year war broke out in Europe. My mother's
family had been through a nightmare in Spain—two of
her brothers had been killed and their little farm had
been destroyed. Madre had an aunt in California who
sent her a ticket to come over to the States. She worked
on her aunt's fruit farm for long, hard months until
her uncle died and the farm was sold off, then Madre
was out of a job and couldn't get one for a long time.
She starved, Quincy. God knows what would have
happened to her if she hadn't met my father. They fell
in love and got married, but my mother never forgot
her first two years in America—she'd been so lonely and
afraid she'd almost turned tail and gone home. If she had
had the fare, she would have done just that, I guess.'

'It must have been terrifying,' Quincy said slowly.
'How old was she?'

'Seventeen when she first arrived, nearly twenty when she married my father. My mother brought us up to remember that it's what you put into life that counts, not what you get out. If you're lucky, you should share your luck. She always said to us: if an apple drops off the tree into your hands, cut it in half and give one half to someone else. Never be greedy with life, be grateful. I think Madre half expected the bad times to come back one day and she was afraid we wouldn't be prepared to face them if she didn't warn us.'

'Who was us? Have you got brothers?'

'Two sisters, a brother,' Joe said.

'Are they older or younger?'

'I'm the eldest—next comes my sister Juana who's married and has a baby girl, then there's Maria who's a commercial artist working in San Francisco, and the baby of the family, Tony, who helps Dad with the oranges. I've put a lot of my money into the estate, we have quite a big spread now. When I'm through singing, I plan to retire and grow oranges myself.'

She was so interested in his family, so intrigued by imagining him at home with them all, that she forgot everything else, and the sudden peal of the doorbell made her jump. Joe's face changed, too, the warmer, smiling expression going and a frown replacing it.

'Who can that be?' he asked with a steely intonation which surprised her until he added: 'If your boy-friend has come back he can just vamoose again—I'm serious about that, Quincy. We can't have him hanging around.' He turned on his heel and strode out of the room with Quincy scurrying after him, her face uncertain.

'Don't you hit Brendan again!' she threw after him,

but when he opened the door it was to find Carmen Lister on the doorstep. She gave him a surprised stare. Quincy distinctly saw a cynical gleam in her eyes and stiffened angrily.

'Well, well, fancy seeing you here,' Carmen said sweetly, walking past him and giving Quincy a considering glance which ran down over her as though Carmen was wondering what any man would see in her. Quincy flushed under that look, grinding her teeth impotently. She knew she was far from being beautiful and she didn't pretend to be sophisticated, but she did not enjoy having Carmen Lister's knowing gaze informing her of the fact. 'So,' Carmen went on, 'Joe found you at last. We'd begun to wonder if you'd bolted for home.' She wandered into the sitting-room and gave it a brief, dismissive stare before looking back at Quincy. 'Don't do a disappearing act again, sweetie. You gave us a headache and caused a lot of bother.'

Quincy resented the patronising tone, and would have said so very succinctly, had Joe not spoken first.

'Have you rearranged your plans again, Carmen?'

She looked at him and nodded. 'The photographer will be along later.'

'What for?' asked Quincy, and Carmen looked back at her.

'I want some shots of you and Joe together, before Joe has to rush off to rehearse. Try to get it into your head, darling—Joe's a very busy guy with a hectic schedule and if you throw a spanner into the works you can ruin everything. Just stay put from now on, and be available if we need you.'

'She understands,' Joe said before Quincy could flare up again at the curt, peremptory tone. 'Quincy,' he went on, 'I'm dying for a cup of coffee, could you make one?'

'Of course,' she said in surprise, and turned to leave the room. As she put the percolator on the stove she heard Joe close the door and frowned. What was he saying to Carmen that he did not want her to hear? She was tempted to go over and listen at the keyhole, but her sense of her own dignity wouldn't allow her to stoop that low. She glared at the closed door, though, feeling like kicking it down, and Carmen's voice rose, wicked with cynical amusement.

'Have you been making little Miss Jones feel more at home, darling? Aren't you clever? Keep her eating out of your hand until we're through with her, will you?'

Quincy turned and walked stiffly into the bedroom and stood there, biting her lower lip to stop herself from bursting into tears, her hands clenched at her sides. That was what he had been doing, was it? She wasn't surprised, she had suspected as much, of course, but he kept surprising her, puzzling her. She could not make him out. At times those dark eyes glowed with a real emotion, it seemed, and his deep husky voice held genuine feeling. When he talked about his home, his family, how he felt about his singing—she could not help believing him. There was such conviction in his face—but then hadn't she been totally convinced by his apparent exhaustion last night, only to find herself being skilfully and expertly seduced? How did she make him add up? He was so unlike any man she had ever met. She could not stop thinking about him, drifting off into daydreams about him whenever she was alone, yet she knew no more about him today than she had the day she first set eyes on his face in that magazine. He had told her so much, apparently laid his life open to her, yet everything he said seemed followed by a question mark. Did he mean what he said? Was he straightforward? Or was he acting all the time, telling her what he thought would convince her and seduce her into trusting and liking him?

She heard the coffee bubbling in the percolator and hurried out of the bedroom to switch it off and find cups. When she carried the tray through she found Carmen sitting down with a sheaf of paper on her knee and Joe leaning against the window, watching the traffic passing the building. He turned and came to take the tray from her. Quincy looked into his face, searching it for some clue to his real nature, but the strong structure defied the probe of her stare. Joe's features kept their secret, the contradictions of his facial strength and that potent male beauty unyielding.

She poured his coffee and he stood talking to Carmen while he sipped it, then he put down the cup, sighed and squared his broad shoulders in a tired way. 'I'll have to be on my way, I guess.'

'Wait just five minutes for the photographer, Joe,' Carmen pleaded, and he glanced at his watch.

'If he doesn't get here within three minutes, I'm going,' he told her.

'He'll be here,' Carmen assured him, and only a moment later the doorbell went and she jumped up. 'I'll get it—it will be Phil.'

She came back with the photographer and Joe told the man: 'I've only got five minutes to spare, so make it snappy.'

The man looked around the room and grimaced. 'This the only background you've got?'

'Yes,' Joe said shortly. 'Get on with it.'

The man gestured to the couch. 'Could we have you both on that?'

They obeyed, Quincy feeling so nervous she had to force a smile, Joe far more casual but obviously with half his mind elsewhere. The photographer posed them, moved around them snapping away, then got them to stand near the window, then near the fireplace, calling out pleas for them to smile or hold hands or look at each other.

'That's it,' Joe said abruptly. 'I must go.' He turned and strode to the door with Carmen hurrying after him. Quincy lapsed into dull silence and the photographer strolled around her, desultorily taking pictures as though he automatically used his camera when he had nothing else to do.

Carmen came back alone and nodded to the photographer. 'Okay, Phil, that's fine.' She picked up her shoulder bag and pushed the sheaf of papers into it before looking at Quincy. 'Just remember, we want to be able to get in touch with you at a moment's notice while you're here, so no more unscheduled jaunts around town, okay?'

When she had gone Quincy sat down heavily and sighed. Her mind was in a confused jumble, but one thing she was certain about—when she got back home she was going to take her brother by the ear and tell him clearly what she thought of him and his great ideas. If he had never filled in that form and put her name on it she wouldn't be in this mess now. Bobby was a pest and she meant to tell him so.

Brendan rang an hour later and as soon as she heard his voice she began to stammer apologetically. 'Brendan, I'm sorry, I didn't mean to hurt your feelings, I shouldn't have said that, it wasn't true . . .'

'It was,' he said wryly. 'I was as mad as fire at the time, but when I'd had time to cool down I realised you were only telling the truth. Aldonez is bigger than me, I can't pretend he isn't. How could I fight a man built like a concrete mixer?'

Quincy laughed, relaxing. 'I'm so relieved you aren't still mad at me—I thought you would be hurt, and I couldn't blame you if you were.'

'Not so much hurt as rueful,' Brendan confessed. 'It served me right for tangling with him—I'll know better next time. I'll sneak up behind him and club him down.'

She giggled, hearing the dry self-mockery in his voice and liking him the more for his ability to laugh at himself.

Sobering, Brendan said: 'Don't get involved with him, will you Quincy?'

Her hand curled tightly around the receiver. 'What sort of idiot do you think I am?'

'He's a very attractive guy and you're not exactly worldly wise,' Brendan told her. 'You could get hurt and I'd hate that, you're much too nice to get tangled up with someone from that sort of world.'

'Do me a favour!' Quincy said lightly. 'Credit me with having some common sense, Brendan. You know I was reluctant to come up to London and go through with this, but what could I do when Bobby had got me into it? I felt partly responsible. After all, it was my brother who filled in that form and by the time they had realised it was all a mistake they'd gone ahead and told the press I'd won. I could see why they wanted me to go through with it. It would have been very embarrassing for them. But I'm taking it all with a pinch of salt, I'm not letting any of the glamour get to me.'

'I hope you're not,' said Brendan, and she heard in his voice the echo of her own doubts, the doubts she had suppressed just now. The glamour might not be getting to her, but how could she hide from herself that Joe Aldonez was?

'They don't want you to stay in London,' Quincy said reluctantly.

Brendan was furious at once. 'I don't care what they want! And by they you mean him, don't you? Aldonez? I saw the way he was reacting. He was dying to punch me on the jaw from the minute he saw me. You could see it in his eyes. He's a nasty piece of work, and I don't like the way he looks at you.'

Quincy's lips parted, the question: how does he look at me? hovering on her tongue, but she carefully didn't ask it, although her heart had given a strange, excited little flip at what Brendan had said.

'Remember,' Brendan charged on angrily, 'he's used to having women swoon at his feet. I'd say he's pretty ruthless about getting what he wants, he wouldn't be where he is if he didn't have a ruthless streak. You have to be tough to make it to the top in any business, but particularly in show business, because the obstacles are higher. A man like that goes like a bulldozer for what he wants.'

Huskily, Quincy said: 'He doesn't want me! Don't be idiotic!' She waited on tenterhooks for Brendan's reply—it was absurd to think Brendan had seen anything in Joe's face that she hadn't seen herself and he was probably putting a false construction on Joe's temper when he saw her and Brendan together, but she couldn't help her inner excitement at what he was saying.

'Don't be naïve,' Brendan said shortly. 'Don't you

know some men notch up their score as if they were going for the world record?'

She changed colour, flinching.

'Quincy,' Brendan said more gently, 'men are different from women. They can separate sex and love—I don't think women can, they get emotionally involved every time. Men just enjoy making it with any pretty girl they meet—some men, that is, men like Joe Aldonez. It's an ego trip for a man like that, part of their image. Don't let him fool you, that's all.'

'I won't!' she said fiercely.

Brendan was silent, as though the feeling in her voice had reached him, then he said: 'Do you want me to stay away? Shall I go back home?'

'After coming all this way to London that would be silly,' Quincy told him. 'Why don't you enjoy a few days here?'

'But I won't see you?' Brendan said flatly.

'I'll be very busy,' she explained in anxious apology. 'And I'll be coming home myself in a couple of days, remember.'

'Yes,' he said. 'I see—okay, Quincy, see you back home.'

She only realised he had hung up when the phone began to whirr softly. With a sigh she replaced the receiver. Talking to Brendan made her realise that this brief trip to London had altered something in her drastically—she wasn't the same girl who had opened the front door to Joe Aldonez so short a time ago. Too much had happened too fast. Her mind was in a state of restless motion all the time. She couldn't sort out how she really felt or what was happening to her. She only knew she had changed, but she had not changed so much that she could bear to contemplate the idea of letting Joe Aldonez use her for an ego trip, as Brendan called it. What Brendan had just said was bitterly close to what she suspected herself—Joe's interest in her was that of the acquisitive collector. He wanted to notch her up on his belt, add her name to his score. Quincy had no desire to be one of a long list of women who had passed through his bed. For the rest of her stay in London she would have to make that very plain to him.

CHAPTER SIX

IT had not occurred to Quincy that she might be present at Joe's big London concert. She knew the tickets had been sold out within a day of the concert box office opening; fantastic, inflated prices were being paid for them on the black market and it was the major event of the pop world in London that year. When Carmen told her she was going she had been so excited she couldn't speak for a few minutes, and an amused look flashed across the other woman's face.

'Lucky girl, aren't you?' Carmen would be there, of course, but she did not appear to feel any particular excitement, perhaps because she was used to big concerts. 'All your friends are going to be green with envy!'

Quincy took it for granted that she would be sitting in the audience, but when she arrived at the hall several hours before the concert began she found she was to be backstage, to her surprise.

'I suppose all the seats were sold,' she said, and Carmen gave her a dry smile.

'Of course, but that isn't the reason—your face would be recognised by Joe's fans and you'd be mobbed. I wouldn't put it past some of the more violent ones to take the chance to scratch your eyes out.'

'Is that why I had to wear dark glasses?' Quincy asked, frowning, and Carmen nodded. She had smuggled Quincy into the hall through a back entrance, but even so they had had to run the gauntlet of a squealing, pushing mob of teenagers and the driver who had brought them had used strong-arm tactics to force a passage for them, flinging back girls out of their path with ruthless disregard for courtesy.

Joe was already there, behind locked doors, in his dressing-room, resting in privacy until the moment when he would have to walk out on stage. Carmen took Quincy through a maze of dark, narrow passages to a cupboard-like room and left her there with a pile of paperbacks and magazines and a radio. 'Amuse yourself, we'll let you know if we need you,' she said as though talking to a child, and Quincy made a face at her departing back.

The hours seemed to drag after that. Quincy skimmed through a book, listening to music on the radio, but her mind refused to stay on what she was reading, it kept wandering and she was annoyed by the direction it always seemed to take. However oblique and indirect her path, her mind always managed to finish up with thoughts of Joe Aldonez. She despised herself.

Carmen came back with Billy Griffith, who was as abstracted as ever. He never seemed quite certain who she was, but he shook hands and told her he hoped she would enjoy the concert.

'Just stay out of everyone's way,' Carmen commanded. 'Stand where you're put and don't budge.'

'Yes,' said Quincy, mentally grimacing at the
schoolmarm tone.

They took her along another set of winding, gloomy
passages and she emerged on the huge stage to find
herself being totally deafened by a sound like nothing
she had ever heard—crashing tides of voices fell on her
from all directions. She was just behind a heavy dark
curtain, and a thin man in shirt-sleeves and wearing a
hectic expression drew a chalk mark on the bare boards
for her to stand on, reminding her to stay on it. 'Don't
move an inch!' he implored, as Carmen had done, then
rushed off without another word.

'This is the warm-up group,' Carmen told her. On
stage, in the spotlights, a group was performing.
Quincy could get a distorted view of the stage through
the curtains, the young men in the group in profile,
the loud thud of their beat making the floorboards
tremble. She could see the vast audience in the hall,
tier upon tier of faces glimmering in shadow, the
brightness of their eyes like glowworms at night, and
she could sense the electric excitement burning in them
as they waited for their idol. It came over in waves to
her, a tension distinctly sexual, as though they com-
municated it to each other and intensified their own
emotions en masse until they took form almost visibly,
so that Quincy felt the audience was one pulsating
creature.

'Joe will be coming out soon,' said Carmen. 'I have
things to do, I'll be back. Stay right there, remember.'

She vanished, and Quincy was not sorry to see her
go. As she stood there, hidden, listening, she felt her
own excitement mounting with that of the audience.

She was so tense her skin was ice-cold and her hands were stiffly curled at her sides, their palms wet with perspiration.

The microphone was taken by a compère, when the group had left the stage. A smiling man in a blue velvet jacket, he began giving Joe his big build-up, his words punctuated by screams from the audience. Quincy felt herself becoming just as excited and looked around behind stage, wondering where Joe was and how soon he would appear.

Suddenly the huge building was vibrating with hoarse yells, tidal waves of sound. Joe was walking out into the dazzle of light on stage. Hysteria broke loose and a forest of arms rose to greet him, waving as girls leapt up and down, beside themselves in their ecstatic delight.

The large orchestra began to play, a line of backing singers at the microphones quite close to Quincy began humming, then Joe's smoky, sexy voice took up the song and the hysteria died down a little as the audience sank into their seats to hear him.

For Quincy that concert was a revelation of the reality of Joe's life—he had such personal impact, such power and strength, yet as she stood there, watching him alone in that blue-white spotlight, facing the vast cavernous blackness of an audience so large that she couldn't guess how many were out there, he seemed suddenly small, very human, very lonely. The hypnotic sound of his voice only just held the audience hysteria in check and between songs their wild shrieks battered his isolated figure like primitive winds. Quincy felt the need in the audience reaching out to engulf Joe and almost shrank from it herself. No wonder he seemed drained after a concert, no wonder he had fled after

the last one, exhausted and depleted, every ounce of
his formidable energy taken from him.

At some stage during the evening, Carmen joined
her again for a few minutes. She was flushed and
elated, looking quite unlike her usual self, Joe's electric
performance having got to her, too.

'Isn't he sensational?' she said, forgetting her usual
cynical cool self. 'They're eating him!'

Quincy shuddered at the image—yes, she thought,
how lethally accurate that is—the audience was eating
Joe, devouring him like some pulsating leech draining
his life-blood.

As the concert went on their excitement mounted to
an incredible high, the waves of sound from them filling the great hall until Quincy was deafened, stunned
by the noise. She could see the sweat dewing Joe's
brown skin, the dampness of his silk shirt, the way the
material clung to his perspiring body as he went on
giving out with everything he had, the high voltage of
his performance making the air crackle around him.

It was a long time before that audience was prepared
to let him go, he kept going off and coming back on
again to do 'just one more' and from his performance
you wouldn't suspect how tired he must be, he had
been lifted by the audience, carried by their excitement
to a succession of peaks.

When he went off for the last time Quincy stood
listening to the shrieks and stamps until at last the
audience began to leave, shepherded out by the uni-
formed security men who had kept guard on the stage
during the show to stop fans from invading it.

She ran into Carmen and Billy Griffith with a group
of other people a moment later, and was drawn along
with them to Joe's dressing-room. He had had a shower

and was wrapped in a black towelling robe, his long legs bare, the dark hair on them damp as was the thick black hair on his head. His eyes were deep exhausted wells, but he was still very high after the concert, laughing with friends, talking to people, a glass of whisky in his hand.

Quincy slid into a quiet corner, hemmed in by strangers, out of Joe's sight. She was tired, too, and kept yawning. She wanted to go home and get some sleep, but she had to wait until Carmen could get her out of the building safely. The fans were jammed around the hall, guarding every exit, the animal roar of their presence reaching the dressing-room.

She leaned her head against the wall, listening to the talk. The room was overcrowded and short of oxygen, far too warm. She got sleepier and sleepier, her lids drooped and her body slackened.

Inside her sleep-heavy mind Joe performed again: moving like a dark fantasy in a glittering spotlight, trapped in a dream.

'Quincy! Wake up!'

His voice seemed part of the dream, she did not break out of her sleep, only smiled faintly, until his fingers brushed along her warm cheek, awakening the pulses slumbering in her body.

Her nerves jerked, her lids rose, she drew a painful breath as she looked up into the watchful eyes.

The dressing-room was empty. They were alone and Joe was very pale under his tan, shadows beneath his eyes, a weary expression dominating his face.

'Where is everyone?' Quincy asked huskily, sitting upright and feeling the sting of pins and needles in her feet as she shifted them after the hour or so she had sat still there, deeply asleep.

'All gone,' Joe muttered on a half-groan of relief. 'Carmen will be back in a minute to smuggle you out. You won't be frightened, will you? The crowd is still out there, but you'll be okay.'

'What about you?'

'I'll hang on here for a while—most of them will go after a while.' He was talking slowly as if each word cost an effort from his tired brain.

Carmen came into the room. 'Ready?' she asked. Her face was pale now, and irritated, weariness hanging over her, too, and, when Quincy did not move immediately, she snapped: 'Well, come on, for heaven's sake! I haven't got all night!'

Quincy got up and Joe's hand briefly touched her fingers, the tiny contact making a spark leap between them, a flash of reassurance which she took with her during the frightening minutes while she and Carmen fought their way through the crush outside. Quincy had been disguised with dark glasses and a headscarf, but she was petrified by the noise and the sheer density of the crowd which pushed and struggled around the building. Policemen forced a way through to a car for them, they climbed in and drove away slowly until they were clear of the hall and fed into the London traffic going back towards the river.

'It's terrifying,' Quincy muttered, huddled into a corner of the back seat.

'You get used to it,' Carmen shrugged indifferently, but Quincy knew she never would—she marvelled to think of Joe facing scenes like this everywhere he went in the world. It must need great courage to walk out on to that stage each time. Having been through it with him tonight she could sympathise far more with his own need for some comforting contact afterwards, understanding fully what had made him come to her that night, in Lilli's flat. He had just done a series of concerts, he must have been totally flat, used up, half dead.

Lilli was in bed when she got back to the flat. She let herself in and went to bed, too. Nightmares kept waking her up—always the same, the crowded hall, the terrifying screams, the reaching, imploring hands from the dark. Each time she lay, trembling, in the darkness of the small bedroom, listening to her sister's rhythmic breathing, envying Lilli her ability to relax like that. How did Joe sleep after a performance? How long could he keep up tours like this one? He surely couldn't enjoy it?

She slept late next morning and found Lilli gone and the flat empty, for which she was rather thankful. She did not have the energy to talk to anyone this morning, she thought, sitting over her morning coffee in the silent room.

It was her last day in London—tonight she would be having dinner with Joe, followed by dancing at a small but exclusive night club, and tomorrow she was going home.

Perhaps it was because she was still tired after last night that she felt so depressed—ever since she came to London she had been wishing she was back home, yet this morning the prospect of returning did not make her want to dance and sing, it made her feel as though her heart was made of lead.

When the doorbell went she started violently, putting a hand to her head as it began to thud. Slowly she dragged herself to the door and opened it. Her spirits were not exactly lifted by finding her visitor was Carmen Lister, wearing a very chic dark grey two-

piece suit of smooth woollen material under which a
white lace blouse showed. Giving her a brisk smile,
Carmen advanced, talking as she came. Quincy could
see she was in a businesslike mood and that it would
be a mistake to argue with any of the plans Carmen
had made.

'Now, we have a lot to do today to get you ready for
the evening. Beauty parlour again—hair, face, manicure. I'll come over an hour before Joe is to pick you
up to make sure you're looking good. We'll be taking
photographs throughout the evening.' She paused,
eyeing Quincy impatiently. 'Well, aren't you ready?
Come on, I haven't got all day, you know, you seem to
have no sense of time at all.'

Dragged at Carmen's chariot wheels, Quincy was
carried across London to the beauty parlour, left in
the capable hands of the young man who had taken
charge of her the first time, and after several hours was
collected again by Carmen. At any other time, Quincy
would have been able to enjoy the fun of it all, but she
found it hard to enjoy the experience under Carmen
Lister's contemptuous, dismissive eyes. Carmen made
it too clear that she was trying hard to make a silk
purse out of a sow's ear.

The dress she was to wear that evening had been
chosen by Carmen, and Quincy herself would never
have thought of wearing anything so revealing or so
daring. When she was dressed she stared at herself in
the mirror, pink to her hairline. She could not go out
like that! She felt half naked. Lilli wandered into the
room and halted, whistling.

'Wow!'

Quincy gave her an anguished look. 'I can't wear it,
Lilli! I feel so conspicuous!'

'Exposed would be a better word,' Lilli said, and laughed. Quincy did not think that was funny—it was too close to the truth.

The dress was made of a clinging white crêpe and was seamless, one huge swathe of material which had been designed to flow over the body like a second skin. Her shoulders were quite bare, the bodice beginning with a fold of black and gold gauze around her breasts, skimming the smooth lift of her flesh just above the nipples, a matching belt of plaited black and gold around her waist, from which the white gown fell softly to her feet.

Quincy did not know herself as she gazed at her own reflection. The dress seemed to give her a height she had never seemed to have—the delicate, stiltlike black and gold plaited leather sandals she wore increased the impression. Her chestnut hair had been set in soft feathery layers which clung to her skull, emphasising the fine bone-structure of her flushed face, and her green eyes glittered between thick black lashes. Tonight Quincy looked tall and slender, elegant, very sophisticated.

'Stop worrying,' Lilli scolded, shaking her head with amused affection. 'You look terrific—what a marvellous dress! I couldn't believe my eyes when I came in just now—you're a real knock-out, you'll cause a sensation.'

'I don't want to cause a sensation!' wailed Quincy.

'Don't be an idiot! All you have to do is put your chin up, look as cool as a cucumber, and if you haven't got the self-confidence of a duchess tell yourself you have and you'll sail through the evening.'

'You're used to being stared at,' Quincy said gloomily. 'I'm not.'

'You can get used to anything,' her sister told her. 'Where's Joe Aldonez taking you, anyway?'

'The Ritz,' said Quincy, and Lilli whistled again, her face full of intrigued amusement.

'I wish I was going to be there to see it.'

'You'll probably see the photographs,' Quincy said, her mouth turning down at the edges. 'Carmen Lister and her photographer are coming everywhere with us, it seems.'

'How romantic,' Lilli said drily. 'Hardly a candlelit dinner for two, then, is it? More like a circus.'

'Why do you think I'm not looking forward to it? I shall feel like a clown.'

'You certainly don't look like one,' Lilli assured her. 'Quincy, believe me, you look fantastic.'

The doorbell rang and Quincy stiffened, biting her lip. 'That will be them.' Her hands curled at her sides, her nails digging into the soft skin of her palms as she grimly considered her reflection in the mirror. How would Joe look at her?

'I'll go,' said Lilli, paused, came back and gave her a quick kiss. 'Remember, you look beautiful.'

'Thanks, Lilli,' Quincy said gratefully. She needed all the confidence-boosts she could get tonight. Lilli walked out and the door opened, followed by Carmen's high clipped tones. Quincy turned slowly and reluctantly to leave the room. She found herself face to face with Joe as she came out of the door. He was frowning as she appeared, but the frown vanished and his face tightened as he looked at her. Quincy could not read his expression. He looked at her with a blankness which defeated her attempt to guess at his reaction.

'There you are!' said Carmen. 'Give her the flowers, Joe.'

Joe's hand came out holding a small cellophane-wrapped box. Quincy automatically took it and the flashlight of the photographer exploded in her face, blinding her. When she could see again she looked at the spray of flowers inside the box, forcing a smile.

'How pretty!'

'Take them out,' Carmen commanded. 'Joe, pin them on her, would you? That would make a nice shot.'

Quincy's fingers fumbled helplessly with the lid of the box. Joe leaned forward and removed it for her, scooped out the spray of pink orchids, and, holding them, moved closer. Quincy looked down, her lashes drooping against her hot cheek, as his fingers took a fold of her gown so that he could pin the flowers to it. She stood frozen in intense awareness as his cool fingers brushed the warm flesh of her half-exposed breasts. He was standing so close to her that their bodies almost touched, she heard his breathing above the ragged sound of her own. The photographer took pictures, moving around them. Through her lashes Quincy took in the elegance of Joe's evening clothes; his wide shoulders smoothly filling a beautifully tailored jacket, his long legs moulded by the matching trousers. His shirt was white, a ruffle of fine lace tumbling down the front of it, which gave him something of an eighteenth-century look, and which emphasised the brown, sun-tanned skin and the jet of his eyes.

'The car's waiting outside,' Carmen reminded them as Joe stepped back, having adjusted the flowers to his satisfaction.

'Have a good time,' said Lilli with a certain sarcasm in her voice, and Quincy gave her sister a drowning, pleading look.

Joe intercepted it, his brows meeting. As they left he
let Carmen and the photographer go on ahead and
slowed his own stride, murmuring to Quincy: 'What's
wrong? Nervous?'

She gave him a quick look. 'Scared stiff—do we have
to have that photographer hanging around all evening?'

Joe frowned again. 'I'll speak to Carmen,' he said as
they came out into the street.

A silvery-blue limousine stood in the yellow lamp-
light and a chauffeur in a peaked cap and dark uniform
saluted as he opened the passenger door for them.
Quincy was helped into the back by Joe amid further
flashlit excitement, the photographer darted around
the car clicking away like a computer.

They drove through streets shining with a sudden
spring rain, the windows of the limousine spattered
briefly before the rain stopped, the tyres hissing as they
moved over the wet road surface. When they climbed
out in front of the Ritz, Quincy's eyes skipped down
Piccadilly, which was ablaze with lights, faintly
blurred by the recent rain, the street lamps glimmering along the edges of the park which was plunged
into darkness, the trees whispering in the wind. Joe
took her arm, his fingers warm, and guided her into
the hotel entrance.

Nervously Quincy walked beside him up the short
flight of steps into the elegant Edwardian atmosphere
of the Palm Court bar, her eyes absorbing the streaked
pink marble of columns, the potted palms and gold-
leaf decorations which were reflected in enormous
mirrors giving the spacious room an impression of even
greater width. The head waiter greeted them with a
smile, led them to a table at one end of the room, and

Joe seated Quincy on the brocade-covered couch, seat
ing himself beside her. Champagne in a silver ic
bucket was waiting for them, the bottle masked by
white damask napkin.

'Shall I open the champagne now, sir?' the waite
asked. A tall, elegant man with black hair, he gav
Quincy a friendly smile as he poured the straw
coloured wine into her glass, but although she smiled
back she was still too aware of Carmen and the photo
grapher to relax. Joe waited until the waiter had moved
away, then leaned forward and said to Carmen: 'That'
enough for the moment, isn't it? Why don't you tw
come back in an hour and get a few pictures of us a
dinner, then we can enjoy our meal in peace?'

Annoyed, Carmen began: 'But . . .'

'Off you go, Carmen,' Joe interrupted, his tone firm
and, with a scowl, she walked away with her photographer at her heels.

Quincy gave a long sigh of relief. Joe's dark eyes sli
sideways, amusement in their depths. 'Feel better?' h
asked with a slight mockery behind his voice, as though
Quincy's nervous dislike of being watched was foolish
No doubt it was, she thought, as she sipped her champagne and let her gaze wander around the room, bu
she couldn't relax while she was conscious of th
photographer, whose antics had already attracted fa
too much attention to them. The bar was crowded, al
the other tables already occupied, and she saw severa
well-known public faces, but although people had
clearly recognised Joe this was not the sort of place
which encouraged clients to make a public display or
show curiosity in any of the famous guests. People
politely looked away, pretended not to have noticed
them.

The tables were small, topped with grey-streaked marble, with pink velvet-upholstered chairs around them. One side of the rectangular room was dominated by a small fountain whose centrepiece was a rocky edifice surmounted by golden figures, naked nymphs and mermaids, with fretted green ferns around the base.

'How do you like the Ritz?' Joe asked, watching her over the rim of his glass.

'It's very ornate,' Quincy said doubtfully.

He laughed. 'The décor is a mixture of Art Nouveau and Baroque. The hotel was built seventy-five years ago. César Ritz was a Swiss who already had a luxury hotel in Paris—both of the Ritz hotels were built to give the same air of timeless elegance. One day you must see the Paris Ritz—you can eat your dinner in a beautiful little walled garden, with fountains playing, and white statues standing under plane trees—it's a very romantic setting. They have a pianist playing Gershwin in the bar and stars in the sky . . .' He grinned at her, wicked teasing in his face.

'You can order the stars from the menu, I suppose,' Quincy retorted.

'At the Ritz you can get anything you want,' Joe mocked. His glance moved sideways to touch the waiter refilling their glasses with champagne. 'Isn't that so, Mr Michael?'

'Certainly, sir,' the waiter agreed with a twinkle.

'Even stars in the sky?' Quincy demanded, and he bowed.

'Whatever my lady wishes,' he assured her, but added: 'I am sure Mr Aldonez does not need to look at the sky for stars while he has my lady's beautiful eyes to look into.'

Quincy began to giggle and he moved away, laughing. Joe sipped his champagne, watching her. 'Not so nervous, any more?' he asked and, with a surprised face, she shook her head. Although the hotel was so luxurious and stately she found it had a relaxed atmosphere which made her feel at home almost at once.

'When you come to New York, you'll find the Plaza very much like this,' Joe told her as they looked through the menu and chose their meal. 'I prefer hotels like the Plaza to the more modern skyscrapers—there's a more human atmosphere. In the huge modern hotels I feel like a battery hen!'

When they were told that their table was ready in the dining-room, they walked along the cream and gold gallery, on smoothly textured floral carpets, into the candlelit shadows of the famous Ritz dining-room. Quincy looked up at the ceiling, painted blue to represent a summer sky, with fluffy white clouds here and there, and an ornate chain of heavy gilt flowers suspended from it in a great oval ring like metal Christmas decorations. On the pink damask tablecloth stood pink carnations, and giant mirrors threw back a swimming reflection of herself and Joe, their faces dim in the candlelight. She crossed her fingers under the table. Please, she thought, don't let Carmen and that photographer come for a long, long time. She wanted to cherish this romantic interlude, to be alone with Joe in the candlelight, for as long as possible. It would be the last memory she would carry back with her to her home. She would never see him again after tonight, but at least she would have a wonderful memory to keep for ever.

CHAPTER SEVEN

CARMEN and the photographer reappeared just as they were finishing their meal and took some more pictures before joining them at the table to have coffee, after which they all left and drove to a night club where they were given a small table in a private corner. The photographer took a few more shots of Joe and Quincy dancing on the shadowy little dance floor, then he left, and a few moments later Carmen went, too. Quincy and Joe stayed. People stared and whispered, but nobody quite liked to speak to them. Joe's dark eyes took on a remote expression if they happened to pass over a stranger. Quincy would not like to be anyone daring enough to risk his anger by approaching them— although he smiled down at her with a gentle mockery, somehow he managed to look very formidable when he was looking up.

'When do you fly back to the States? she asked while they were sitting at their table drinking some more champagne.

'Tomorrow,' he said.

She looked into her glass to hide the stiffness of her smile. 'I expect you're looking forward to getting home.'

'Yes.' His voice was clipped. 'And you?' he asked. Are you longing to get home, too?'

'Oh, yes!' said Quincy with an extreme enthusiasm which, to her own ears sounded slightly phoney. Ever since she got to London she had been telling herself

how much she wished she had never left home, and
now, with her return to the security of her family close
at hand, for some unaccountable reason she felt like
crying. She drank some more champagne, but it had
little effect other than to make her spirits sink ever
lower—maybe it was the champagne which was making
her want to burst into tears like a child and stamp her
feet, she thought. What else could it be?

Through her lowered lashes she peeped at Joe and
found his face in profile to her, the gleam of the brown
skin lit by candles, his nose an arrogant sweep above a
hard, fierce-looking mouth. Her heart plunged as he
turned his head towards her and put a cool hand on
top of one of her own.

'Shall we dance?'

As they got up the music changed to a slow, dreamy
waltz and Joe drew her into his arms, one hand curving
around her slender waist, the other clasping her fingers
loosely. The floor was crowded, they had to dance
slowly, almost at a shuffle, their bodies so close that
Quincy felt the warmth of his thigh against her, com-
municating a restless heat to her skin and making her
stomach tighten in unwilling attraction. Never before
had she ever been so conscious of a man's sexuality. A
slow-burning fuse had been lit inside her and she was
growing lightheaded as it fizzed through her body. Joe
moved, shifting closer, his arm tightening around her
waist. She felt his long fingers just below the uplift of
her breast, his body warmth penetrating her thin silky
dress to make her own skin prickle with awareness.

'Still sorry you agreed to come to London?' he
murmured, his lips close to her ear, the feel of his
breath against her skin.

A trembling sensation started inside her, as if she

had swallowed a butterfly which was fluttering around in an attempt to escape.

'I suppose not,' she said huskily. She kept her eyes lowered, afraid to look at him, because the drastic things he was doing to her heartbeat had frightened her. He was too attractive, it was dangerous to let herself meet those wicked dark eyes which were gleaming like jet through his lashes.

'You look beautiful tonight,' he whispered. She felt his lips graze her ear, follow the delicate convolutions of it with tactile sensuality.

Before she could pull away, or protest at that, she felt his mouth softly sliding down her throat and her pulses went crazy.

She reminded herself that his intentions were strictly dishonourable, he was only amusing himself with her, and if she let him go on with this gentle seduction she would find herself in a situation which could only lead to heartache for her.

Her throat hurt, dry with aroused excitement, but she made herself say: 'I think we should go now, it must be getting late and I have to get up early to catch the train home.'

She half expected Joe to protest, but he led her off the floor without a single word, and within ten minutes they were back in the waiting limousine and driving back to Lilli's flat.

It wasn't until the car had pulled up and she was climbing out of it, her head bent, carefully lifting up her long white skirts to avoid treading on the hem, that Quincy realised that they had not returned to Lilli's flat at all. They were outside Joe's hotel. She turned at once, alarm in her face, but the limousine had begun to glide away and she walked straight into Joe.

'What are we doing here? I want to go back to my sister's flat!' she protested angrily, her head lifted to stare at him.

'The night's still young,' Joe said smoothly. 'I thought we'd have a peaceful nightcap together before I took you back.'

'Do you think I'm stupid?' Quincy retorted, bristling with alarm and anger. 'I'm not going up there with you—get that car back and take me home, or I'll get a taxi!'

'I've ordered some supper for us,' he said. 'Carmen and the photographer are waiting to take some final pictures.'

Quincy stared at him, her eyes uncertain. Was he telling the truth?

He gave her a mocking little smile. 'What a suspicious mind you have!' His hand curled round her arm and he led her into the hotel before she had time to consider what she should do, walking with her to the lift, talking softly in the hushed night-time atmosphere of the hotel lobby.

'I'd rather go straight back to Lilli's flat,' she said weakly as the lift door closed on them and they climbed to the floor on which Joe's suite was situated.

'Relax and enjoy yourself,' said Joe with a smile that took her breath away. She looked down nervously, alarmed by her own response, knowing her heart was beating like a wild tattoo inside her chest and her body was trembling.

When they reached the suite he pushed open the door and Quincy walked past him. The rooms were dark and empty. As Joe flicked down the light switch, she turned on him angrily.

'You lied! Carmen isn't here!'

'Isn't she?' Joe asked, but as Quincy darted back towards the door his arm barred her way. 'Where are you going?'

'I'm not staying here alone with you!'

'Why not?' he asked coolly, holding her. 'What are you scared of?'

The question choked back the flood of furious words which were about to burst out of her. She glared up at him, her green eyes glittering. He knew very well what she was worried about! There was taunting amusement in his face, he was daring her to admit that she was afraid that he might seduce her, and such an admission would be dangerously revealing. Joe could only succeed in seducing her if she wanted him—by admitting that she was afraid, she was admitting that she was attracted to him.

'Why did you lie to me? You knew Carmen wasn't here! You didn't arrange for any final photographs!'

His mouth twisted sardonically. 'I wanted to bring you here and I knew you wouldn't come unless you thought we wouldn't be alone.'

'That's despicable!' Quincy flung at him.

He shrugged and her eyes nervously watched the little movement, made aware by it of the power of the slim body under that elegant dark suit. The smooth tailoring could not hide the strength of his muscled chest—Joe Aldonez was a tough customer, for all his charm, a man whose face could look as if it had been carved out of granite. Quincy stiffened, hearing the silence of the empty suite beating around them, reminding her that they were alone, and that if he used force she would not be able to do much about it.

'I'm not in the habit of forcing myself on women,' he said, as if he read the thought in her eyes. 'You've no need to shiver in your shoes.'

'I'm not shivering in my shoes! I just don't like being lied to,' said Quincy, her chin raised defiantly. 'Will you take me home, please?'

He turned her towards the sitting-room, his arm controlling her, and said: 'Come and have some supper first.'

'I'm not hungry!'

He said so softly she only just heard him, 'Quincy, don't make me angry! This is our last evening together, don't spoil it.'

She was silent, a quiver running through her. Heat burned behind her lids, she swallowed on a lump in her throat, afraid she was going to cry. She barely knew him. Why on earth should she feel like bursting into howling tears?

He took off the little fur jacket she wore and gestured to her to sit down on the brocade couch, then picked up the phone and rang room service. 'We'll be ready for our coffee in ten minutes,' he told them, and put down the phone.

A cold buffet had been left on a table for them. Joe put some blue-green quails' eggs on a plate, added some caviar, and brought it to her with some wafer-thin curls of cold toast.

'I'm not hungry,' Quincy insisted.

'Try a quail's egg,' he said, and went back for some of the food for himself.

Quincy hesitated, then decided that a pretence of eating the food would at least keep them safely occupied until she could again insist on being taken home. She nibbled at a tiny egg, bit into a thin crisp of toast. Joe poured her some champagne and she refused to drink it. She had already drunk far more than she normally did and she knew she was lightheaded with the wine. She needed to be more clearheaded than usual right now, she did not want to go floating in a golden bubble of champagne-induced happiness. The whole evening was taking on the appearance of a dream—she looked back on it dazedly, her senses assailed by a dozen glamorous memories of chandeliers and flowers, candles and champagne, music and shadowy rooms.

The coffee came and she took hers black—it might wake her up, pierce the bubble of excitement she had been trapped inside. It did not seem to have much effect. Each time Joe leaned forward, or shifted beside her, she felt her nerves quivering with reaction.

When he took her cup out of her fingers, she sat stiffly upright. 'I really must be going!'

He put the cup down and, as she rose, fastened his fingers around her wrist and jerked her back.

'Don't!' Quincy said hoarsely, too late, and found herself pulled on to his lap. Her head whirled as she was tilted backwards against his arm. The champagne was making her dizzy, she decided, grabbing at his shoulder to steady herself. 'I don't want you to touch me,' she muttered, knowing her face was glowing poppy red.

'Liar,' Joe whispered, bending towards her, and his lips grazed gently over her flickering lashes, forcing her to shut her eyes. It was rather restful, she felt, as the light of the room vanished. Joe's lips glided right down her nose and she began to giggle, wriggling on his knees, until they reached their intended destination and closed over her parted lips. As she felt the hard, male mouth take possession of her own her body was wrenched by a sense of need that took her by storm.

Her hands went round his neck, her body curved towards him, and with a helpless, restless sigh of pleasure she met his kiss with a hunger which matched his.

She had known perfectly well that if she stayed here alone with him, this would happen—Joe's intentions had been obvious to her ever since the night he spent on the couch in Lilli's flat. He was a sophisticated man who had travelled all over the world and had presumably forgotten most of the women who had lain in his arms like this—his teasing, arousing kisses had been learnt with experience, whereas Quincy was entirely untutored, her mouth softly submitted to him with an innocence she couldn't disguise from him. Desire was mounting inside her like some elemental force she had no idea how to control; her husky little moans of pleasure stifled by Joe's searching mouth.

'I need you,' he whispered hoarsely, his lips wandering down her throat to explore the warm cleft of her white breasts, and she shook like a leaf at the sound of his voice, her eyes closed to shut out the light, her hand lifting to stroke his tumbled hair as his black head burrowed into her.

'You're so warm and soft, I want to hold you in my arms all night and wake up feeling you close beside me,' he said, his hands moving in slow, seductive caresses that sent her temperature climbing. She was lost in a burning sensuality, abandoned to the wild fevers of a desire she had never known before, wanting him so much it was like dying, an extremity of passion which held her speechless and helpless in his arms.

When a sudden blinding light exploded close beside them she was too dazed for a second to think. Her lids fluttered as she was broken out of her trance of excitement. The next second she heard Joe's voice swearing thickly and he had leapt off the couch.

Quincy opened her eyes, blinking, so startled she didn't move, staring as Joe broke into a run in pursuit of the man leaving the room.

Quincy just had time to see the camera the other man held before he and Joe had vanished. The sound of their struggle brought her to her feet, swaying, shocked and suddenly icy cold.

Angry voices, a crash, were followed by the slam of the front door of the suite.

While Quincy struggled to pull herself together, Joe came striding back into the room, a camera dangling from his hand. He walked to the telephone and lifted it, dialled. 'This is Mr Aldonez,' he said in a deep, harsh voice. 'A press photographer just broke into my suite and took a picture of me. I want him stopped before he gets out of the hotel and charged with breaking and entering, and I want to know how he got in here. I don't expect to have pressmen wandering in and out of my suite as though it was public property, I don't pay the fantastic sums you charge to have my privacy invaded by anyone who cares to open my door.'

Quincy was feeling sick as she listened. A stranger had come in here and taken a picture of her and Joe— had seen them on that couch, making love. She tugged up her tumbled dress, adjusting the bodice over her half-exposed breasts, shuddering with distaste and self-disgust. What must she have looked like to that man? The thought of someone watching them made her want to throw up.

'Apologies come a bit late,' Joe was saying furiously. 'What sort of hotel is this? What sort of security do you have?'

Quincy picked up her fur jacket and wrapped it
around herself as if the room had suddenly turned cold.
All the hot colour of sensual excitement had left her
face. She was white and drawn, her green eyes full of
bitter realisation. She had come within a hair's breadth
of letting Joe make love to her—another few minutes
and they would have been in bed together. She hadn't
had any intention of stopping him just now. She had
been too wrapped up in sensations of agonising desire
to think of anything but the satisfaction of a need she
had never felt before.

'Get on to it right away,' ordered Joe, and slammed
the phone down. He turned, opening the camera and
removing the film. Quincy watched as he dropped it
into a wastepaper basket and flung the camera down
on to a table. Joe stared at it, his mouth a grim, hard
line. 'The guy himself got away,' he said tersely. 'If
I'd caught him I'd have broken his neck, so it's
probably just as well.'

Quincy couldn't speak.

He looked up and stared at her, his brows dragging
together as he took in the expression on her face.
'Don't look like that!'

'How do you expect me to look?' she whispered, the
sound issuing from between her lips like a dry haze of
smoke, so low he had to bend forward to hear her.

'I'm sorry it happened,' Joe said.

'So am I.' Her lips moved in faint irony, trying to
smile, but only succeeding in trembling slightly.

'You see what sort of thing I have to expect,' said
Joe. 'It's a professional hazard, it happens all the
time.'

Quincy looked at her watch. She didn't really see
the time, although she stared at the little gold face, the

minute hands fixed briefly at some hour. 'I must go,' she said politely, as if they were strangers. 'My sister will be worried about me.'

'Quincy——' Joe began abruptly, taking a step towards her, and she shrank involuntarily, her hands clutching at her jacket, her head lowered.

Joe halted in mid-stride and stood there, his eyes on her averted face. She heard her own heart beating in a sick, ragged rhythm and, above it, the deep uneven sound of Joe's breathing.

He suddenly turned towards the door. 'Okay, I'll drive you home,' he said as he walked away. Quincy followed him unsteadily out of the suite and down the corridor to the lift. Joe didn't say a thing as they made their way through the hotel. Around them hung a sleeping hush, the sound of their footsteps seeming too loud, and, as they got down to the lobby, the man at the reception desk looked up and got to his feet with a concerned expression.

As he started to speak, Joe shook his head at him. 'I'll be back later,' he said curtly, and steered Quincy out of the door into the chilly air of the spring night.

The limousine was parked along the street. As they walked to it, Quincy glanced up miserably at the sky and saw the pale points of light glittering remotely far above them, the stars unhidden by cloud tonight in this cold, clear weather. The fine silver disc of the moon had a silent eloquence which deepened her sense of misery, making her even more aware that she would never see Joe again, that the brief days she had spent with him in London were over, were ending in a fashion that lanced her with pain. She would never be able to forget either her own hectic abandonment in his arms, or the shock of being wrenched out of it by the intrusion of a curious, prying stranger. It seemed to encapsulate the whole situation—underline both the unreality of her relationship with Joe and his public situation.

Joe Aldonez was not an ordinary man—he lived in public, like some golden icon, always watched by fascinated eyes, and his emotions and thoughts were as much public property as his singing. He had no right to a private life of his own, as far as the press were concerned. Quincy did not want to live like that. She remembered her sense of his isolation, as she watched that concert last night, seeing him in the dancing, blinding spotlight, trapped like a moth in the glare of a radiance which held all eyes. Then she had seen his humanity, his loneliness, but now she saw other things. How could he not be aware of always performing under watching eyes? And how could his emotions have any depth, any reality, when he must constantly guard himself? Joe was not physically inhibited, but there must be a mental inhibition, a shield lowered between him and the world.

Joe put her into the passenger seat, walked round and opened the driver's door. She sat in a huddled silence as he started the engine, staring straight ahead. The car drew away from the kerb and turned out of the side-road. Without looking at her, Joe said: 'I understand how you must feel, you know.'

'Do you?' Her lips were dry and barely moved as she spoke.

'I live in a goldfish bowl. Do you think I enjoy it? When something like this happens I get so mad my head nearly blows off.' His powerful hands flexed on the wheel and he muttered: 'If I'd got my hands around his neck I'd have choked him to death!'

Quincy stared at the empty silent streets through which they were driving. No doubt it happened to him all the time—how often had he begun to make love to some girl only to have a sneak photographer pop up at an inconvenient moment?

Joe swung the car down towards the river and she caught a glimpse of the moonlit water glimmering between high buildings. London was asleep around them, scraps of torn white paper blowing along the pavements, the traffic lights ahead turning red as they approached and looking to her like dangerous, glowing eyes in the dark. She shivered and Joe shot a sideways look at her.

'Cold? The heater's on, the car should warm up pretty soon.'

'I'm okay,' she said in a stiff voice. She wanted to get away from him, be alone, where she could nurse this pain out of his sight. She wasn't even sure how deep it ran or where it had its source—whether what was making her want to cry was simply the shame she felt at having been seen by a stranger in Joe's arms, or whether the shame came from a realisation that in so short a time she had come so close to giving herself to a man who, tomorrow, was going to fly out of her life for ever.

The car drew up outside Lilli's flat a few moments later. Joe turned towards her, his arm resting on the wheel.

'There's so much I haven't had a chance to say to you,' he began huskily, but Quincy interrupted, forcing a smile.

'I really must go in, Mr Aldonez—it's getting so late.'

'Quincy——' he began angrily, and she turned and

fumbled with the door, ignoring the note in his voice.

'We can't leave it like this!' muttered Joe, catching her shoulder, trying to turn her to face him again.

'We've got nothing to say to each other,' said Quincy. 'I just don't want any part of your sort of life, I'm not your sort of girl. I couldn't live in a goldfish bowl. I've hated every minute of the publicity—I wish I'd never said I'd do it. I wish I'd never come to London at all!' Without waiting for him to answer she wrenched at the door, it opened and she almost fell out on to the pavement and scrambled away, flinging a smothered 'Goodbye' at him as she ran.

She half expected to hear him following her, but the click of her high heels was the only sound disturbing the silence of the sleeping street. As she reached the door she heard the limousine throb into life behind her, then the wheels swished on the road surface as it moved off, and she turned her head, briefly, to see the tail lights disappearing before she went into the building.

She was far too disturbed to sleep. She quietly made herself some coffee and sat curled up in a chair, brooding, her body shivering in a convulsive way from time to time, as though she had an intimation of some fatal disease. The room gradually lightened around her, a pale cold light filtering through the drawn curtains. Towards seven o'clock she heard Lilli getting up and uncoiled to stand up just as her sister drifted through the door in a dressing-gown, yawning.

Lilli halted, falling without thinking into one of her elegant dancer's poses, her slender body slack from sleep but innately graceful. Opening her eyes very wide, she asked drily: 'How long have you been back? I went to bed at one and you weren't back then—what have you been up to, Quincy?'

'I haven't been up to anything!' Quincy flared at once, knowing she had gone pink.

'What an interesting colour!' Lilli drawled, and her smile was amused. 'Joe Aldonez made a night of it, did he?'

'We went on to a night club,' Quincy admitted. 'But I've been back for hours. I wasn't sleepy.'

'You haven't done anything silly, have you?' asked Lilli in a different voice, a frown pleating her forehead.

'Of course I haven't—what do you mean?'

Her sister stared, visibly hesitating. 'He's so different from the men you usually meet,' she said. 'I wouldn't want you to get hurt.'

'I'm not stupid,' said Quincy, wishing it was true—she was stupid, that was the trouble, she had to be to have allowed herself to get involved with Joe in the first place.

Lilli ran a hand over the ruffled feathers of her vivid red hair, smoothing them down. 'A pity I've been so busy with rehearsals, I meant to keep a closer eye on you, I promised Dad I would.'

'Did he ask you to?' Quincy bristled, very offended. 'Anyone would think I was ten years old! I'm twenty-two, remember! I don't need to have anyone keeping an eye on me.'

'Quincy, I'm used to men like that—you're not, you don't realise what rats they can be . . .'

Oh, don't I? Quincy thought, but she said nothing, merely looked mutinously at her sister and shrugged.

Guiltily, Lilli said: 'Sure nothing's wrong? You can talk to me, I won't repeat it—if something's bothering you . . .'

'It isn't,' Quincy said succinctly. 'If you're trying to find out if Joe Aldonez seduced me the answer's no, he didn't.'

Lilli made a wry face. 'That's it, be blunt!'

'Well, that was what you were hinting at, wasn't it? Why wrap it up?'

'I didn't want to put ideas into your head,' said Lilli with amusement. 'I wasn't sure you already had them.'

'As I've said, I'm twenty-two, not ten—I do know the facts of life, I don't still think babies are found under gooseberry bushes.'

Lilli laughed. 'I never did—Dad explained to me when I was about six and first noticed that one of the cats he had in the surgery was looking strangely fat.'

'Yes,' said Quincy, remembering, 'he put me in the picture at around that age, too.'

'He's cunning, our father,' Lilli said, and Quincy felt suddenly so homesick she wanted to burst into tears. She couldn't wait to get home and feel the warm, loving security closing around her again.

'I must have my bath,' Lilli said. 'I'm being picked up at eight-thirty, we're rehearsing all day again.'

'You work too hard,' Quincy told her.

'Don't I know it? This morning I feel as if I've been put through a mangle, every bone in my body is aching.'

'Do you still think your career is worth it?' Quincy asked her curiously—Lilli, like Joe, lived in the public eye and, like him, had to give all her time and energy to the pursuit of fame. Why did they do it?

'At the moment, no,' Lilli said frankly. 'Ask me after we've finally recorded the show and I'll probably say something quite different.'

Quincy was silent as her sister walked away, then called after her: 'Want some coffee?'

'Love some,' Lilli groaned. 'I need something to wake me up!'

Quincy made the coffee, listening to the radio, and, as she was getting herself a slice of toast to go with it, heard the telephone start to ring. She hesitated for a moment, half afraid it would be Joe, then when Lilli yelled from the bathroom: 'Get that, will you?' slowly went to answer it.

It wasn't Joe, it was Brendan, sounding tentative and uncertain. 'Quincy? Hallo, I wondered if you were going back today by train or . . .'

'Yes, I am,' she said.

'So am I—we could travel together.' He made the suggestion shyly.

'What train are you catching?'

'The one at eleven,' said Brendan, still clearly expecting a refusal, and Quincy said in a bright voice: 'Great, that suits me.'

'Oh,' he said, and there was a brief silence. 'Shall I pick you up in my taxi?'

'Thanks,' said Quincy, 'I'd love a lift,' and Brendan rang off, telling her he would be there at ten o'clock. As Quincy put down the phone and turned, she found Lilli behind her, a towel tucked around her and her shoulders gleaming wet.

'Who was that?'

'Brendan—we're going back home together on the train. He's calling for me at ten—I must get my case packed.'

'Nice guy, Brendan,' Lilli said enthusiastically, and Quincy gave her a wry look, understanding perfectly why her sister had assumed that lively tone. She might have denied to Lilli that she had got involved with Joe, but Lilli was too shrewd to believe her. Her warm support of Brendan came too patly to be real—Lilli was waving Brendan at her like some consolation prize, which wasn't very fair to him. Brendan was far too nice to be treated as a runner-up and Quincy had no intention of doing that, she did not want to hurt him any more than she wanted to get hurt herself.

Lilli left an hour later and, hugging her warmly, gave her a string of messages for their parents. 'Tell them I'll be in touch,' she said finally, as she left, making Quincy frown. What would Lilli tell them about this trip?

Her sister caught the apprehension in her gaze and grimaced at her. 'Oh, no need to look worried—I'll be discreet. They won't hear anything from me that they haven't heard from you.' She shrugged. 'Not that I know anything to tell, I'm in the dark as much as they'll be.'

'About what?' Quincy demanded, and got a sardonic smile.

'About whatever you're not telling!' Lilli retorted, and was gone before Quincy could burst into agitated denials.

Brendan arrived punctually at ten and carried her case out to the waiting taxi. Quincy climbed into it and Brendan told the driver which station they wanted—but, as they settled back in the car, another car shot round the corner, almost colliding with the taxi. Quincy gave the driver a cursory glance, recognised him and did an alarmed double-take that matched the one he was giving, his black head screwed to stare at her as he parked the long limousine on a double yellow line, indifferent to the beady eye of an offended traffic warden who came marching back towards them, pad in hand, the light of battle in her face.

'Do you want to talk to him?' Brendan asked her, staring at her hotly flushed face.

'No, I don't,' said Quincy, and he leaned forward to tell the taxi driver to drive on, just as Joe leapt out of his car and sprinted towards them. The taxi throbbed, drawing away, and Joe jumped on to the running board and glared at the driver.

'Hold on!' he shouted, and the man slammed on his brakes.

'What d'you think you're doing? You crazy?' he demanded as he turned towards Joe.

'I want to have a word with your passenger,' said Joe, pulling a five-pound note out of his pocket and flinging it to the driver, who automatically grabbed it, looking startled.

'Well, sir, all the same, you shouldn't jump on the running board while I'm moving, you could get killed doing things like that,' he scolded.

'Sorry,' said Joe, and gave him a hurried smile. 'I wasn't thinking.'

'It's Mr Aldonez, isn't it? I've just been listening to you on the radio,' the driver said, and Brendan with a face like thunder got up and pulled the window down to say: 'We're in a hurry, what do you want, Aldonez? Quincy doesn't want to talk to you.'

'I want to talk to her,' said Joe, appearing close beside the window. His eyes bypassed Brendan to find Quincy and she looked away, sitting stiffly in the far corner. 'Quincy, I must talk to you!'

'*I* want to have a word with *you*,' said the traffic warden behind him. 'You can't park that car on a double yellow line, you know that perfectly well.

Kindly move the car immediately and park in a legal parking space.'

Joe ignored her, all his attention concentrating on Quincy's averted face. 'I haven't got much time,' he said huskily.

'Don't you know when you're not wanted?' Brendan asked him, getting a black stare in reply.

'Here, you!' said the traffic warden, tapping Joe on the shoulder. 'Are you listening to me?'

'Wait a minute,' he muttered without looking at her.

'Who do you think you're talking to? Some people have a nerve! Just because you're driving some car worth a fortune you think you can ignore traffic laws, don't you? Well, you can't, mister. I don't care who you are, you're not parking on a double yellow line in my zone!' She was scribbling on a sheet of paper as she talked and Joe's head swivelled to watch her as she stalked over to his car and stuck the ticket under his windscreen wiper. Arms akimbo, she gave him a triumphant glare. 'And if you haven't moved it in five minutes, it'll be towed away to the police car pound,' she promised with every sign of extreme satisfaction.

'You know what you are?' Joe roared, striding back towards his car. 'If there's one thing I can't stand it's petty bureaucrats in uniform!'

The taxi driver, sympathetically excited, stuck his head out of his window to watch. 'Put a woman in a uniform and what do you get? Mother Hitler,' he commented.

'Are you parked there or are you taking those people somewhere?' the traffic warden demanded before her attention was distracted by Joe, who, with a savage expression, had snatched the ticket from his windscreen and was ripping it to shreds and throwing the little fragments up into the air. 'Here! I suppose you think that's funny?' she shrieked, turning on him.

'No,' Joe snarled. 'I'm not in the least amused, madam.'

Brendan leaned forward and tapped on the glass between them and the driver. 'We're in a hurry, drive on.'

The man threw a look back at Joe, hesitating, remembering the five-pound note he had been given.

'We'll miss our train if we don't go now,' urged Brendan, and the man shrugged.

Quincy sat, cold and miserable, in the corner as the taxi moved off, hearing Joe's voice behind them. 'Quincy!'

She knew what he had wanted to say to her, she didn't need to hear it. Joe had come to say goodbye, but she had already said it to him in her heart, it didn't need saying aloud.

CHAPTER EIGHT

QUINCY might have imagined that in leaving London behind she would also be escaping from the attentions of the press, but, as she discovered when she got out of a taxi outside her home, she was sadly mistaken. A flashbulb exploded, almost blinding her, as she turned towards the gate, and the next moment a young man in a leather jacket was giving her a coaxing smile and asking breathlessly: 'How does it feel to be back home, Quincy?'

Still dazed after the surprise of the flashbulb, Quincy

automatically said: 'Fine,' before she halted, her mouth open.

'What was it like having a date with Joe Aldonez? Will you be seeing him again? What did he say to you?'

Since she made no attempt to answer any of the questions, merely stared at him, going crimson with growing rage, he rushed on to the next one, apparently in the hope of startling some sort of answer out of her. 'What happened when you had dinner with him?'

Brendan had paid off the driver and was manhandling the cases out on to the road. Taking in what was going on, he dropped them both and took two rapid steps, grabbing the young man by his collar.

'Here, what're you up to?' the reporter gurgled as Brendan bundled him away from Quincy. The photographer took a couple of quick pictures before he fled to their waiting car. Brendan frogmarched the reporter after him and bawled: 'And don't come back!' before he returned to join Quincy, who had taken advantage of his rescue attempt to flee towards the house. The front door opened and her mother smiled at her.

'Mum!' Quincy almost wailed, on the point of breaking into childish tears, and Mrs Jones looked sharply at her, her smile vanishing.

'Whatever is the matter? Is it those journalists? They've been hanging about all afternoon, I told them to go away but they took no notice. I should have called the police. Did they pester you?'

'Yes, they started on her the minute she was out of the taxi,' Brendan answered for her as he hauled the cases through the door.

'I've got the kettle on,' Mrs Jones said excitedly. 'Come and have your tea and tell me all about it—I'm dying to hear every detail.'

'I'm tired, Mum,' said Quincy, and out of the corner of her eye caught Brendan shaking his head at her mother.

'I'm sure you are,' Mrs Jones said more soberly. 'That train journey takes it out of you, I know whenever I get back from London I feel worn out.' She was looking at Quincy searchingly as she talked and Quincy avoided meeting her eyes. While she was in London she had rung her family several times, but on the phone it had been easy to elude difficult questions. Face to face, it wouldn't be so simple, she was afraid of what she might betray. She had pretended to go to sleep in the train, which had kept Brendan at bay, but unless she was going to imitate the Sleeping Beauty and stay in her bed for the next few months sooner or later she would have to talk to her mother.

'I'll have to go and check up on my patients,' said Brendan, vanishing towards the surgery, and Quincy rather regretted his disappearance. She could have used Brendan as a shield, but, once they were alone, she was going to have to face her mother without defence. She had never needed to hide from her mother in the past and she found it painful to need to do so now, but then she had never before felt an emotion she did not want her mother to suspect. Her life until now had been an open book, she had never learnt how to disguise her feelings, nor had she ever before had feelings so powerful she was afraid to let them be glimpsed by anyone.

In the kitchen the kettle had begun to boil with shrill insistence and Mrs Jones ran to snatch it up and make the tea.

'Your father's out on his rounds,' she said as she

covered the pot with a knitted patchwork cosy. Staring at it, Quincy remembered making it while she was at school. The gaudy red and yellow wool had faded with washing and the lining was showing through. She stared as intently as though she had never seen it before while her mother talked. 'We've kept every one of the papers, your father got them all every day. Wonderful pictures of you—I've started a scrapbook of them, but there were so many pictures I haven't had time to stick them all in.' She put the teapot on the table. 'I've got some scones in the oven, they'll be ready in a minute. Wait until Bobby gets home from school, he's dying to hear all about it. His friends have been badgering him . . .'

'That's nothing to what I'd like to do to him,' Quincy said grimly.

'Why, what's he done now?' his fond mother asked without sounding very surprised at the threat in her daughter's voice.

'He got me into all this,' Quincy muttered.

Her mother shot her a look. 'Didn't you have a good time, Quincy?'

'Don't ask,' Quincy begged. 'I can't face talking about it at the moment—you've no idea what a trauma the whole thing was!'

Mrs Jones didn't seem anxious. 'I suppose you're not used to so much excitement, but when you look back on it you'll be glad it happened,' she said calmly.

That's what you think, Quincy thought, as her mother got the scones out of the oven and tipped them out on to a cooling tray.

The phone rang and Mrs Jones said absently: 'Answer that, will you, Quincy? Don't forget, your father's out, but Brendan is in the surgery.'

Quincy looked at the phone with nervous loathing.
'Could you answer it, Mum? It might be the press,
and I really can't face the idea of talking to them.'
Secretly, she suspected it might be Joe, and her desire
not to talk to him was a good deal stronger than her
dislike of talking to the press.

Her mother wiped her hands on her pinny and went
across the room to pick up the shrilling telephone.
'Hallo?' She listened, then smiled. 'Oh, hallo, Penny
dear, how are you? How's the baby?' She paused, eyes
bright, then said, 'Is he? Well, at that age they get
everywhere, the minute they can walk they're swarm-
ing all over the furniture.'

Quincy snatched a hot scone and dropped it on her
plate, blowing on her fingers.

Her mother turned and held out the phone, 'Penny
to speak to you,' she said, and Quincy went over to
take the call.

'Hello, star!' Penny teased, and Quincy grimaced to
herself.

'Hallo,' she said warily. 'I gather David is on his
feet at last.'

'Unfortunately,' Penny groaned. 'I was so thrilled
two days ago. He took one tottery step and fell flat on
his nose, and I was over the moon, but since then he
refuses to stay put anywhere. He screams if I try to
put him in his pram and insists on practising for the
marathon all over the house. I can't take my eyes off
him in case he gets out into the farmyard and is eaten
by the ducks.'

'I'd be more worried about the ducks if I were you,'
Quincy said, and her friend laughed.

'You're so right! Anyway, what about your adven-
tures? Don't think we haven't been kept informed.

Along with the whole village we've been following your rake's progress with fascination.'

'Everything that happened has been publicly chronicled,' Quincy lied, hoping she sounded convincing.

'Everything?' queried Penny, sounding far from convinced.

'Absolutely everything!'

'I don't want to call you a liar,' Penny began, and Quincy interrupted.

'Glad to hear it!'

'But,' Penny went on, overriding her, 'I don't believe a word of it. Come on, Joe Aldonez spent a whole evening with you—he must have said something that didn't get into the papers.'

'If he did, it was by accident,' said Quincy. 'I think our table was bugged. Maybe they missed the odd word, but not much else.'

'Why do I get the feeling you're holding out on me?'

'Nothing to hold out on,' Quincy said firmly. 'I'll be over to see you soon, I can't wait to see David legging it for the wide open spaces.'

'All right,' said Penny with an ominous note in her voice, 'I'll talk to you then.'

Quincy hung up and turned to find her mother observing her with shrewd, bright eyes. Flushed, Quincy went back to butter her scone while it was still warm, and while she was drinking her tea her father came into the kitchen, his skin glowing from a battle with the spring wind, his hair ruffled and his stride forceful.

'You're home!' he said, coming over to hug her and rub his cold cheek against hers. 'Everyone in the district has been talking about you, they're dying of curiosity. Suddenly you're famous. How does it feel?'

'Terrible,' she said frankly. 'And before you start asking, yes, I had an exciting time in London and yes, I'm very glad to be home, and no, I don't want to talk about it. At the moment all I want to do is forget it ever happened.' She got up and walked to the door. 'I think I'll have a bath,' she said over her shoulder as she left the room, aware of her parents staring at each other behind her.

They discreetly asked her no further questions when she drifted downstairs an hour later. Bobby, however, was not so easily silenced and fired a positive volley of questions at her when he got back from school. Since he was largely interested in knowing what sort of car Joe Aldonez had, how fast it went and what Quincy had eaten at the dinner party, however, she found it comparatively harmless to face his quiz. Bobby did make a hooting comment on one or two of the pictures which had appeared in the papers.

'You looked pretty daft when you were dancing with him in that night club, but I suppose you couldn't help that, girls are always swooning over pop stars.'

'Not this girl,' said Quincy, grabbing his ear. 'If you hope I've gone soft at the centre, you can forget it, Bobby Jones. I haven't forgotten who filled in that form.'

'Ouch!' he yelped, squirming away. 'I've got homework to do—'bye!' He vanished up the stairs and a moment later the usual heavy thud of rock came from his room as he settled down to a quiet hour with his books.

'His transistor has packed up altogether,' Mrs Jones said thoughtfully. 'Next time I'm in town I'll have a look at radios and see if I can afford a new one for him.'

'Masochist,' Quincy said affectionately.

'Well, he's a good boy,' his mother insisted, and Quincy gave her an incredulous smile.

'Who, him? Mother darling, may you be forgiven!'

'He could be worse,' Mrs Jones defended.

'By what stretch of the imagination do you work that out?' Quincy demanded, prodding the vegetables cooking on the stove.

'He works hard at school and he's very careful with the money he earns with his paper-round.'

'You mean he's a miser,' Quincy agreed. 'Yes, I think he's got more in the post office bank than I have.'

'That's not fair!' Mrs Jones fired. 'He bought me a very pretty ornament for my birthday, he's very thoughtful.'

Quincy gave her an amused smile. 'All right, we'll agree—Bobby's an angel, all he needs is some wings.'

'And a new transistor,' her mother said, chuckling.

That was to arrive two days later. The parcel was addressed to Bobby and caused much excitement in the house as it stood in the hall waiting for him to get back home from school. Mrs Jones was dying to know what it contained, pinching it and brooding over it every five minutes, until Quincy suggested she should open it as she was so fascinated.

'Of course not, it's addressed to Bobby,' her mother said, going pink and marching away.

The minute Bobby came through the front door he spotted it with his usual lynx-like keen sight. 'What's that?' he asked, falling on it with unhidden curiosity before he even realised it was addressed to him. 'It's for me,' he announced, grabbing it up, as his mother and Quincy arrived on the scene.

'We weren't going to snatch it away,' Quincy retorted. 'It's been driving Mum mad all day—for heaven's sake, open it!'

Nothing loath, Bobby attacked it and his mother squawked: 'Not like that! Come into the kitchen, I'll find some scissors for that string.'

While Bobby danced impatiently around her she carefully snipped the string and then wound it into a neat little ball which she slid into her string drawer, rescuing the brown paper as Bobby began to disembowel the package in his brutal fashion, too eager to get at the contents to care how he did it.

When the last wrapping fell away and the polystyrene box was unveiled Mrs Jones and Bobby gazed at it blankly—Quincy had long ago guessed what the package held. The address had been typewritten and there was no letter inside. The transistor had come anonymously as far as Bobby was concerned. Lifting it reverently out of its box, he gave a long happy sigh.

'Oh, wow!'

Mrs Jones looked at her daughter, her face flushed, her eyes very bright. 'You're a naughty, extravagant girl,' she said, and hugged her.

'I didn't send it,' said Quincy, and Bobby detached his adoring gaze from the radio's shiny chrome dials.

'Who's it from then? It's fab, absolutely terrific, it must have cost a bomb. I bet I could get Mars on it!'

'Who sent it, then?' Mrs Jones asked.

'Joe Aldonez, I expect,' Quincy admitted.

Bobby lit up. 'Really? No kidding? Oh, wow!' he exclaimed, and extracted the enormous aerial which waved high above his head as he twiddled with the wavelength dial. 'Hey, I'm going to have a great time with this!' he informed them as he cuddled the radio against his ear and went off with it on his shoulder like some space age Long John Silver, the squawk of the radio fading with him as he vanished up the stairs.

Mrs Jones was still thinking about what Quincy had told them. 'What makes you think Mr Aldonez sent it?'

'He said he would.' She had forgotten, it had entirely slipped her mind since she came back from London, but Joe had not forgotten, he had kept his word.

'Isn't that nice of him? Isn't he a kind man,' Mrs Jones said in delight, 'When you think how much he must have on his mind it's very thoughtful of him to remember Bobby.'

'Yes,' said Quincy. 'Isn't it?'

'We could never have bought Bobby such a splendid radio,' Mrs Jones went on. 'Bobby's right—it must have cost a fortune, it's very generous of Mr Aldonez. Bobby must write and thank him at once.' She went off to point this out to her son and Quincy stared out of the window at the gathering spring dusk, watching small powdery moths tapping at the lighted window, the brush of their wings insistent as they tried to penetrate the glass.

A melancholy enveloped her and she sighed. She did not want any reminders of Joe around at the moment. She had put away her cherished LP until she felt she could bear to hear it again—maybe one day in the dim and distant future she might be able to listen to that smoky voice without wincing, but right now it would hurt too much.

Over the following weeks she had to hear with patience the sight and sound of Bobby and his radio. They were never parted, and her only consolation was that she could always hear them coming and remove herself from the vicinity before they arrived.

Bobby wrote a thank-you letter to Joe and sent it care of Carmen Lister in London. Presumably Carmen sent it on to America, but Bobby had no reply, not that that seemed to bother him much; however, it did nag away at Quincy whenever she stopped guarding her mind from thoughts of Joe.

Her life had returned to normal, or what passed for normal, so far as everyone around her was concerned. The nine days' wonder of her trip to London over, people stopped talking endlessly about it, to her relief, and the subject was allowed to fall into abeyance. Quincy settled back to work in the surgery, she went for drives on a Sunday afternoon with Brendan and took walks with him through the local woods admiring the spring flood of bluebells which began to carpet the leafy moistness of the earth under the trees, filling the air with that special, poignant scent. Now and then they drove to the nearest cinema to see a film or went dancing in the village hall on Saturday nights. Coming home late they would sit in the car and talk for a few moments before they kissed, and Quincy fought to hide from Brendan that his kiss hardly turned her on, her pulses never so much as fluttered.

Wryly one evening he drew back and looked down at her. 'I'm wasting my time, aren't I?' he said. 'We just don't click.'

'I'm sorry, Brendan,' she began, but he cut her short.

'Don't say sorry, that would be adding insult to injury. If you can't feel any more than that, you can't, and there's an end to it. I don't want you apologising for it.'

'Sorry,' she automatically mumbled again, then gave a nervous little giggle as she caught sight of his face. 'Oh, Brendan, I am—don't scowl like that.'

'Was I?' he asked ruefully, giving a little shrug. 'Shall we call it a day?'

'Friends?' she asked tentatively, holding out a hand.

'Of course,' Brendan said, politely shaking it as though they had just been introduced.

In her bed later Quincy got the giggles again as she remembered that, but under the laughter she felt faintly sad. If she had never gone up to London, met Joe Aldonez, she might have taken Brendan far more seriously, allowed their quiet companionship to move into deeper waters without any sense of haste or strain. Now she had to admit it would never happen—she had changed too much during her brief stay in London, she would never be quite the same again. As with the end of anything, facing the reality of her break with Brendan saddened her and left her feeling slightly lost. Brendan had been a part of her life for the last five years, their friendship recently holding a hint of something else, and she knew she would miss their evenings together, their long walks at the weekend. It had hardly added up to deathless romance, it had been a cosy habit, nothing more—but she would miss it.

As summer advanced towards its peak, the lanes grew creamy with wild parsley, which foamed in the ditches and clambered up the green banks, while the cuckoo sounded distantly across the fields, coming and going with that deceptive cunning which makes it seem invisible, a voice rather than a living bird. On warm, sunny days, Quincy went off with her father on his rounds if she could free herself from the paperwork of the practice, driving around the farflung district in which he worked, from farm to farm, from village to village; sometimes helping out when he needed a spare pair of hands to hold a calving cow, but often just going along for the ride, wandering off during his visits to explore a secret copse or feed an apple to a horse, or lie in the sun in a meadow watching the tiny black shadows of the larks singing high up in the halcyon sky.

One morning in early June they called at Hough Farm and while her father and Jim Stevens went off to the cow shed Quincy sat in the kitchen talking to Penny and her mother-in-law, who was feeding David a bowl of minced beef and finely mashed carrots; much against his will, since his real interest in the food was an intense desire to grab some and watch it oozing out of his little pink fist as he squeezed it, as he demonstrated whenever Mrs Stevens took her attention off him to look at his mother.

'Eat it, don't play with it,' Penny scolded, pushing back a lock of limp hair from her flushed cheek. 'Isn't it hot today?'

Her mother-in-law looked up from cleaning David's sticky fingers, frowning. 'You don't look well, girl,' she said in her soft burring West Country accent. 'Been pushing yourself, I reckon. You don't need to work so hard, take it easy once in a while.'

'I'm just tired,' Penny said, shrugging. 'He's been teething on and off for weeks, I never seem to get a full night's sleep. I sometimes wonder how many teeth he plans on having.' She watched with a wry grimace as David opened his mouth, displaying his present collection of pearly white teeth, and closed it again sharply on the bowl of the spoon and all it contained. Mrs Stevens extracted the spoon with difficulty.

'You wicked little imp,' she told her grandson

fondly, and he beamed with satisfaction, cheeks bulging. 'What you need is a holiday,' Mrs Stevens went on, looking at her daughter-in-law.

Penny groaned. 'Do I not? But Jim can't spare the time from the farm until late autumn.'

'Go on your own,' Mrs Stevens said. 'I'll look after the house and David for you, I'd love to.'

'I can't just dump him on you—you've no idea what a handful he can be!'

'Who hasn't?' Mrs Stevens retorted, looking offended. 'Anyone would think I'd never brought up one of my own. He can't be any worse than his father.'

'Oh, can't he?' Penny said gloomily. 'That's what you think. David is in a class of his own. He doesn't want to be a farmer, he wants to be a demolition expert. If he lives to grow up, that is. Yesterday he tried to eat the flex of my iron. I grabbed him just in time. You have to watch him twenty-four hours a day to make sure he doesn't kill himself.'

'He's tiring you out, and it shows,' her mother-in-law said, shaking her head in disapproval. 'You need a complete break for at least a week.'

'I wouldn't enjoy a holiday on my own,' Penny said. 'And I'd never persuade Jim to leave the farm in midsummer, you know that.'

'His father could manage without him,' said Mrs Stevens, but her voice somehow lacked conviction, and Penny gave her a wry look.

'If you decide to go and need someone to share the costs, I'd love to come,' said Quincy, and Penny looked round at her.

'Are you serious?'

'Of course. I could do with a holiday, myself.'

'Where would we go?' Penny thought aloud.

'Somewhere different and exciting,' Quincy said, and Penny made a face.

'Like Blackpool?'

Quincy grinned. 'Why not abroad? We could have a week in Paris.'

'Too expensive,' Penny said.

'Holland?'

'Too flat—I know I'd spend the whole week buying bulbs to bring back for my garden, anyway.'

'Why don't you get some brochures from the travel agency next time you're in town?' suggested Mrs Stevens.

'You're so practical, Mother Stevens,' Penny said, laughing, but her eyes had excitement in them and her face was lit up. The very idea of getting away from all her exhausting chores had lifted the weary dullness from her face.

A few days later, Penny rang while Quincy was busy measuring out the feeds for the animals being kept overnight, and said excitedly: 'I've got some brochures, want to come over and gloat?'

'Love to,' said Quincy. 'I'll have finished work around three. I'll drive over then—made any ginger cake lately?'

'Cupboard-lover,' grinned Penny, then gave a shriek slightly off telephone: 'David! Don't touch that vase!' There was an ear-splitting crash somewhere in the background followed by affronted bawls of dismay. Penny groaned. 'Too late! I'll have to go—see you later.' The phone clicked and Quincy put down the receiver, smiling. Poor Penny!

She drove over to the farm later that afternoon in tranquil golden sunshine, watching the undulating green curve of the land on the horizon, looking for all the world like some enormous Chinese dragon curled up asleep in the sun. A heat haze danced ahead of her on the road. Dark green elms dreamed in pastures, their shifting, flickering black shadows full of tiny midges. It was the sort of day Quincy remembered from childhood with a dreamlike intensity as coming every day in high summer, but which later experience told her came too rarely.

David was fast asleep in his pram in the garden, a green canopy shielding him from the sun, the white fringes of it fluttering in a breeze. His flushed face had a cherubic innocence, his sprawled body breathed peacefully.

Penny looked at him, grimacing at Quincy. As they went into the farmhouse, she said softly: 'To look at him now you'd never think he was a demon when he's awake. So far today he's poured a cup of milk into Jim's wellies, bitten the dog and smashed my favourite vase.'

'And now he's having a rest before he gets back to work,' Quincy said, laughing.

Penny shuddered. 'I'm glad somebody thinks it's funny—my sense of humour gets mislaid at times. I suppose one day I'll be able to laugh about it, but it took me half an hour to clear up the mess when he broke that vase. Broken glass flies everywhere, I'm still finding splinters of it in the carpet and I dare not put David down anywhere near the hall in case he finds one—he has a perfect genius for finding trouble.'

They sat at the kitchen table, drinking tea and flicking over the glossy pages of the brochures, dreaming of a fortnight in Acapulco or a few weeks cruising in the Bahamas, before they settled down to deciding on something they could actually afford. Neither of them

had much money. Although the farm was highly pro-
ductive, most of the profits were ploughed back into
farm equipment and stock, and Quincy's bank account
was never exactly healthy; she spent most of what she
earned.

'Spain's not expensive,' Penny thought aloud, gazing
at a highly coloured picture of a bullfight.

Quincy stared at it, too, seeing in the black hair and
tanned face of the bullfighter a strong resemblance to
Joe Aldonez. Her mind detached itself and floated off
into memories.

'What do you think?' Penny's voice broke into the
dream and Quincy jumped, eyes opening wide.

'What?'

'Spain, stupid—you aren't listening!'

'Of course I am!' Quincy protested. Joe had talked a
great deal about Spain and although he himself had
never yet been there had obviously been fascinated by
his mother's country. Quincy felt she would like to see
it. She had some vague idea that by visiting Spain she
might get closer to Joe, understand him better. 'Spain
would be wonderful,' she said, searching her mind for
some memory of the name of the mountain village
which Joe had mentioned as the place his mother came
from.

'This is a package deal,' said Penny, pointing to the
brochure. 'Everything included; air flight, hotel, full
board—so long as there are no hidden extras, we could
manage that price, couldn't we?'

'Where is the town exactly?' Quincy asked, not re-
cognising the name of the resort, and Penny got up
and went in search of an atlas so that they could consult
the map of Spain and see exactly where the seaside
town lay. Quincy, under a pretence of studying the

surrounding area, was looking out for the name of Joe's mother's home village.

'What do you think?' Penny demanded.

'If we can book for this hotel, that would be fine by me,' Quincy said absently, suddenly seeing the name she was looking for, and flushing. It wasn't far from the resort at all. They might be able to take a coach trip in that direction, she thought.

'At this time of year it might be fully booked, but we can ask, can't we?' said Penny. 'We'll pick a couple of other holidays to be on the safe side—if I can't book that hotel, where shall I try instead?'

'Where you like,' said Quincy, crossing her fingers secretly. The idea of visiting Spain, now that she had had time to think about it, had made her very excited. She didn't want Penny to guess what was in her mind, though, nor did she mean to mention Joe Aldonez or the fact that he came from a family of Spanish descent. Penny might tease her.

They were lucky—bookings were down because of the recession and the travel agency were able to offer them a choice of dates. Penny booked them for the last week of June to give them a chance to save a little extra money, and to give herself time to get a passport. The week they were leaving the weather turned suddenly and icy winds blew in from the north, bringing grey skies and rain, which made them even happier to be flying away to a promise of sunshine, sea and lazy days on the beach.

Having kissed David and handed him to her mother-in-law, Penny commenced to bewail the fact all the way to the airport; her brow constantly furrowed with anxiety in case the baby fretted for her, or nibbled his way through an electric wire without being detected and short-circuited himself, or, even worse, in case he developed a form of infantile anorexia because of her disappearance and wouldn't eat his strained prunes.

'Do shut up,' Quincy said crossly at last, her patience giving out. 'He's going to be fine, your mother-in-law loves every fat inch of him, and you know it. She'll spoil him rotten! But if you don't stop wailing about it I might very well push you out of the emergency exit on the plane while we're flying over the Channel!'

Penny said: 'I always knew you had no heart,' but shut up obediently, only to start on the subject of Jim half an hour later. 'I forgot to pick up his grey suit from the cleaners, I must ring home and tell them. He'll want to wear it when he goes to the Rural District Council Meeting.'

'The whole object of this holiday was to part you from your problems,' Quincy pointed out. 'Forget Jim and his grey suit, forget David and his prunes—just think about dark-eyed Spaniards with roses in their teeth.'

Penny giggled. 'I'd remind you, I'm a respectable married woman!'

'I said think about them,' Quincy stressed. 'I didn't say do anything more.'

'Who said that sex was ninety per cent imagination?' Penny asked.

'I don't know, who did?' Quincy prompted.

'I don't know either,' said Penny. 'But he had something!'

Having left England in a windy, rainy turmoil they arrived in Spain in the middle of a thunderstorm of operatic proportions and, amidst earsplitting rolls of thunder and zigzagging flashes of white lightning, drove to their hotel in a small coach crammed to the doors with nervous ladies in summer dresses and men in shirtsleeves complaining that they hadn't paid through the nose for weather like that.

Next day, however, the sky was a clear, washed blue and the sun had faithfully returned to give the small resort a glittering white brilliance that brought smiles to the faces of the other guests at breakfast.

'This is more like it, isn't it?' one of the men who had flown over with them commented as he passed their table, and Quincy nodded and smiled back.

They spent the morning on the beach, lying on green-striped mattresses under beach umbrellas, taking the occasional stroll down to the sea and after a swim returning to flop out again like basking seals. Their hotel owned a small part of the beach and at the sea wall there was a café selling cold drinks and ices.

'This is the life,' Penny murmured without opening her eyes as Quincy sat up to lubricate herself with suntan oil again. Her skin felt comfortably warm, flushed with sunshine, but she decided to adjust her sunshade to give herself more shade. It would be stupid to get sunburn, right at the beginning of their holiday. With a sigh she relapsed into torpor and drifted off into a half-sleep full of the sound of the waves, the distant murmur of voices and the feel of the sun beating down around them.

They walked back to the hotel for lunch at one o'clock, strolling in the shade of some trees lining the promenade. Penny suddenly stopped at a small shop selling local, hand-made toys. 'Look at that gorgeous pink bear! I'll get that for David, he'll love it.' Diving into the shop, she left Quincy loitering on the pavement, gazing idly around her at the town. It had been a little fishing port before the advent of tourism; a maze of narrow, shadowy alleys, with small white houses crammed together, on a steep hillside leading to a quay. Now white skyscraper blocks of concrete and glass towered around the old town, choked traffic filling the narrow medieval streets.

A constant drift of people up a side street caught Quincy's attention. She wandered a few steps that way and stood on the corner, watching as the crowd moved towards a large building at the top of the narrow street.

Circular, rising in stone tiers of a creamy pink colour faded with sun and time, the building defeated all her attempts to guess at its function. A railway station? An opera house? she wondered. Gothic arches pierced it at intervals, giving it the likeness of some crumbling wedding cake which has been nibbled by giant mice. The Colosseum in Rome, Quincy thought suddenly— that's what it reminds me of! Obviously the crowds thickening around it were tourists eager to improve their minds before they collapsed on the sun-drenched beach.

Behind her, brakes suddenly screamed, horns blared, and she turned quickly to stare at the road. A white car had swerved out of the bumper-to-bumper lines of traffic and was parking half on the pavement. While Quincy watched, a man leapt out of the car and turned towards her, ignoring the excited invective he was getting from other drivers.

For one second Quincy thought she was imagining things, then as the tall black-haired man loped towards her, the sun flashing off the mirror of his dark glasses, she felt shock clench her stomach. Only one man in the world moved like that.

Agitated panic sent her running in the opposite

direction; forgetting Penny, forgetting common sense, only knowing she could not bear to face Joe again, it would hurt too much.

'Quincy!' His voice held anger, but far from halting her, it made her more determined to get away from him. The very sound of his deep, husky voice made her heart beat fiercely and her skin prickle with anguished awareness.

'What are you *doing* here?' he asked, as though her presence was inexplicable, something he found difficult to believe.

'I'm on holiday,' she said, adding crossly: 'Obviously—what else would I be doing here? What are *you* doing here? I thought you'd be in America.' She wanted to make sure he knew that, it was certainly true, and she didn't want him imagining that she had come to Spain in the hope of seeing him. She might have fallen in eagerly with Penny's idea, but she hadn't suggested it, she could comfort herself with that, and if Spain had been invested with magic because of Joe's family connection with it, there was no reason he should know that and no reason why she should feel guilty.

'I'm taking a holiday, too, would you believe?' said Joe with a trace of derision. 'My manager decided I was tired and overworked and suggested I take a month off, so as my parents have wanted to show me Spain for years, I jumped at the chance.'

'Are they with you?'

'Yes,' he said, smiling. 'They're having a second honeymoon, they tell me.'

'With you along?' Quincy asked, laughing, and saw an answering amusement in his eyes.

'I'm the soul of tact,' he assured her, then his eyes

ran down her slim body. 'Been on the beach?'

She nodded, grateful for the fact that she had slipped a yellow towelling beach robe over her swimsuit before she left the beach. Sleeveless and V-necked, it ended mid-thigh, exposing most of her long, smooth-skinned legs. Against the deep tan of most of the people they had seen since they arrived, both she and Penny had seemed very pale, but her morning on the beach had given her a faint sun-flush. Joe, on the other hand, was as tanned as ever; his skin a deep, golden bronze she envied.

'How are your family?' he asked.

'Very well, thank you.' Their voices sounded stilted. From talking to each other with that painful intensity they had retreated to a polite formality she found almost as disturbing.

'Did Bobby like his radio?' Joe asked, and she could have kicked herself for not remembering to thank him without being prompted.

'He was thrilled,' she said hurriedly. 'It was very kind of you to remember it, thank you very much.'

'It was part of our bargain,' he said, and the curt phrase made her wince, reminding her too vividly that those days in London had been nothing but a publicity stunt to him, part of his career, a business matter. There had been nothing personal about it. He had flirted with her, but it hadn't meant anything to him. In the weeks since they last met he probably hadn't even thought of her once, while she hadn't been able to get him out of her mind. He had lingered like some song you can't quite remember, but can never forget; haunting and troubling you at odd moments of the day. She had carefully avoided talking about him to anyone, in the hope of forgetting; but that had only locked him inside the secret chambers of her memory, he had never left her, she had felt her whole body jerk in tense attention if one of his songs was played on the radio or he was mentioned in a newspaper.

'Are you here alone?' Joe asked, and she looked at him, startled.

'No, I'm with a friend,' she said, suddenly remembering Penny, who would no doubt be wondering what on earth had happened to her.

'I see,' said Joe, his hands dropping away from her. 'Brendan?' The question was delivered in a cool voice, but his face hadn't altered; his dark eyes fixed on her face, watching every flickering expression, his mouth straight and firm and unsmiling.

'Brendan?' she repeated, flushing. 'No, of course not—I'm with an old school friend, Penny Stevens. I was waiting for her just now when . . .' she broke off, her eyes moving away from him. 'She'll be looking for me, I must go before she gets in touch with the police and reports me missing.'

This time Joe made no attempt to detain her. He fell into step as she turned to walk away, his black shadow thrown along the sunlit stone wall as they made their way out of the building, into the blinding glare of the Spanish afternoon. Looking sideways at him as a woman near the gate stared, Quincy murmured in warning: 'You'd better put your sunglasses on before you're recognised.'

He fumbled in his shirt pocket, drew them out and slid them on, becoming at once just another black-haired Spaniard.

'I'm surprised you don't have bodyguards,' Quincy commented and he grimaced.

'In the States I do when I'm travelling from gig to

gig, but I thought I'd be okay over here. I hate going around with a couple of gorillas.'

'I'd hate it too,' said Quincy, and he shot her a hard look.

'Yes,' he said, as though she had not needed to tell him so. 'My mother finds it upsetting. At one time she used to come to my concerts, but it gave her night-mares, she said, so she stopped coming.'

'I don't blame her.'

They had walked down the narrow road leading back towards the sea. In the distance she could see the unreal blue of the water, the cloudless brilliance of the sky above it stretching to where they met on the hori-zon, a picture postcard beauty which had destroyed the little fishing port which had once stood here, and replaced it with palaces of concrete and glass, and arti-ficial green lawns set with islands of gaudy flowers. The tides of holidaymakers flooded in with the spring and out again, no doubt, with the onset of autumn, leaving the town dead and empty and meaningless.

'You'd like her,' Joe said suddenly.

Quincy turned her head to look at him, but the dark glasses defeated her, as always, and she could not de-cipher his expression. 'Who?' she asked blankly.

'My mother—we're staying at a hotel a few miles up the coast, will you come over and have lunch tomor-row?'

They had reached his car and before Quincy could answer they were pounced upon by a tall, olive-skinned policeman who had been prowling morosely around it and who, seeing them halt, swung round to say: 'Ah, señor!' in a menacing tone before commencing a long sentence in Spanish of which Quincy understood not a word but which she gathered was not complimentary.

Joe halted him, a hand on his arm and said something briefly, then looked round at Quincy. 'Where are you staying?'

'The Hotel Madrid,' she said.

'You'll come to lunch tomorrow?' Seeing her hesitate, he added quickly: 'You will, won't you, Quincy? I'll pick you up at noon at the hotel.'

The policeman was listening with a frown, impatience in his face. Quincy sighed and nodded before she walked away, leaving Joe to deal with the offended law.

She was far too late for lunch, the dining-room was empty, and as she let herself into her room Penny sprang out of her own to hiss furiously: 'Quincy, where on earth have you been?'

She turned round, her face contrite. 'I'm sorry, have you been worried?'

'Have I been worried?' Penny repeated, fizzing with irritation. 'I was on the point of declaring you officially missing—what happened to you? Why did you vanish like that? I thought you'd come back to the hotel for lunch and I ran all the way back here only to find you weren't here, either. I didn't know what to think— where have you been?'

'I met someone,' Quincy said, very flushed.

'You haven't let a Spaniard pick you up?' Penny demanded. 'Quincy, honestly . . .'

'No,' said Quincy. 'It was someone I knew.' She couldn't bring herself to confess that she had bumped into Joe Aldonez, although she realised that sooner or later Penny was going to find out if Joe meant to come to the hotel tomorrow.

Penny looked surprised, which was only to be expected, since they had known each other all their lives and lived in a very small community where everyone knew everyone else. 'Who?' Penny asked, obviously searching her memory for the name of someone likely to have chosen Spain for their holiday. As far as Penny was aware, Quincy didn't know anyone Penny didn't know too.

'You don't know him,' Quincy told her, and Penny looked disbelieving.

'I don't? Then who is it?' Suspicion showed in her face. 'You've been holding out on me, Quincy—is he special?'

Quincy hesitated, but the only answer to that had to be in the affirmative, so she agreed. 'Yes.'

'Too special to talk about?' Penny was looking excited now, curiosity vying with sympathy in her eyes.

'Yes,' said Quincy, relieved to be able to tell some of the truth, at least. 'I'm sorry you were worried, I shouldn't have dashed off like that without telling you, but . . .'

'But you just forgot I existed!' Penny said drily, and Quincy laughed and nodded.

'Afraid so—sorry.'

'It must be love,' Penny said, and Quincy almost flinched, hiding it with a pretence of a smile, before she went into her room.

'Did you get lunch?' Penny asked, and she nodded. Although she had missed lunch she wasn't hungry, her mind was too busy with other thoughts, she had no attention to spare for food.

'I think I'll take a shower,' she said. 'I've got a bit of a headache.'

'I've got some more shopping to do,' said Penny. 'I want to get Jim a present. While you're showering, I'll take a walk, okay?'

'Fine,' Quincy said gratefully, and was glad when the door had closed and she was alone. She slid out of her robe, unhooked the top of her swimsuit and peeled it off, then walked into the shower, standing under the lukewarm water with closed eyes, letting the salt wash out of her hair, the trickle of the spray cool her heated skin. Her heart was beating far too fast and her nerves prickled as though she had developed some strange illness, but it was a sickness she had been carrying for a long time, although she had only just admitted it to herself. Penny's casual, laughing words had merely said aloud what she had known when she came back from London—she was in love with Joe, she had fallen in love almost before she saw him, listening to the velvety seduction of his voice day after day. Until she actually met him it had been a dream, a fantasy, a game of love from which she might one day have awoken to fall in love with some other man, someone from her own world, but Joe had walked out of his dream setting and become real to her, turning her fantasy into reality.

She wrapped herself in a large white towel and sat on the stool in front of the dressing-table, rubbing her damp hair and looking at her reflection with dismay. Why had Penny had to say that? She could have gone on for ever pretending that she did not know how deep her own feelings were—but now she had to face them and it hurt, because her love was so stupid, so pointless. Joe could never return it, he would never feel that way about her. He had made love to her in London only because she was there, it had been the automatic reaction of a male instinct and had had no root in emotion, Quincy had known that at the time. Even so hot colour swept up her face at the memory of the night he had come to Lilli's flat, exhausted, and held her in his arms on the couch, naked desire in his dark eyes as he touched her. Perhaps that had been the moment when her feelings had deepened into real passion—the dreamy romanticism had become a burning need as she hovered nervously on the verge of surrender, all the more powerful because it was the first time she had ever felt like that. All that she knew of passion she had learnt that night; Joe's hands had taught her body needs it had never felt before, and ever since she had been aching for that final lesson, longing to experience the intimacy only lovers know.

She dressed clumsily and lay on the bed with the shutters closed, the room in comforting shadow. Her head throbbed with frustration and misery. How was she going to face him tomorrow? How could she talk to him, look at him, now that she knew how she really felt?

Penny came back an hour later and tapped on her door. Quincy forced a smile somehow and agreed to go down to the beach again—anything was better than lying alone in her room with nothing but her own gloomy thoughts for company, and there was no reason why she should let her sudden depression ruin Penny's holiday. Pretending to be cheerful might actually make her feel as if she was—it seemed to fool Penny, why shouldn't it fool Joe?

She slept badly that night and in the morning could scarcely force down her breakfast. 'Aren't you hungry?' Penny asked in surprise, taking another roll and pouring herself some more coffee. 'I'm starving—it must be the sea air.'

'I've got a headache,' said Quincy.

'The sun,' Penny stated. 'I told you it was danger-ous.'

'So you did,' Quincy agreed. Why hadn't someone told her Joe was dangerous in time to save her from the way she felt now? But if they had, what difference would it have made? She had known, she hadn't needed to be told, her own common sense had kept on warning her and she had still gone right ahead and fallen helplessly, stupidly in love with him. Perhaps there is a time and a place when one falls in love, how-ever foolish? Perhaps she had been ripe for love, wait-ing blindly for it, ready to go crazy over the first at-tractive man she saw? How else did she explain the instant insanity of falling for a man like Joe Aldonez?

She wondered how to break it to Penny, or whether to trust to luck that Penny didn't actually see him when he came.

'I've got a date this afternoon,' she said casually, avoiding Penny's eye. 'For lunch, actually.'

'Oh, have you, *actually*?' said Penny, grinning. 'I wondered when it would come out.'

'What?' asked Quincy, confused.

'I guessed you'd be doing another vanishing act some time or other,' Penny explained. 'I suppose you and he planned it? I think you might have told me you'd arranged to meet him here.'

'I hadn't,' Quincy said indignantly. 'It was sheer accident.'

'Pull the other one,' Penny told her cheerfully. 'I wasn't born yesterday. I'm not a great believer in coin-cidences.' She regarded Quincy thoughtfully. 'He isn't married, is he?'

Startled, Quincy said: 'Not as far as I know,' then thought, and said firmly: 'No, I'm sure he isn't.'

'Why all the secrecy, then?'

Quincy hesitated: 'I just don't want to talk about it yet, there's nothing to talk about at the moment, maybe there never will be.'

'Oh,' said Penny, much enlightened. 'Like that, is it? I get you, you don't know where you stand yet?'

'No!' Quincy said. 'I don't know where I stand at all.' And that was the understatement of the year, if only Penny knew. It seemed to satisfy her, though, she asked no more questions, and Quincy left her basking peacefully on the beach when she left to make her way back to the hotel in time to change before meeting Joe.

She blowdried her damp hair while she scrutinised the limited contents of her holiday wardrobe—what should she wear? What would be suitable for a meeting with his parents? There wasn't really much choice, she had not come provided with much beyond beach wear and a few summer frocks. In the end, she put on a silky white dress printed with the occasional trail of green ivy—it looked fresh and springlike, even if it was hardly haute couture. Someone like Carmen Lister might be able to look at it and see at once that it was bought from a chain store, but what did that matter? She slid her feet into high-heeled white sandals, clipped a string of pretty local green beads around her neck and checked her reflection without satisfaction. She was never going to set the world on fire, whatever she wore, but at least she looked cool and assured, on the surface, and Joe would not be able to see beneath that.

He arrived punctually at twelve and rang her room from the desk downstairs. Quincy was pleased with her own calm voice as she spoke to him. 'Hallo, yes, I'll be down right away,' she said, and put down the phone, lifting her chin in defiance at herself in the mirror. Surely she could put on an act for a few hours?

Joe was waiting in the reception lobby, she saw him before he saw her, his arrogant profile masked by those sunglasses, his tall, lithe body lounging casually as he studied a poster on the wall near the desk. Quincy's heart traitorously turned over at that first glimpse of him. You fool, she told herself in disgust, pull yourself together, then he turned and saw her and she saw his mouth curve into an involuntary smile and smiled back, her heart lightening and her nervous tension dropping away.

'You look lovely,' he said, taking the space between them in three strides. 'White suits you, that's a very pretty dress.'

'Thank you,' she said, hoping she did not sound as breathless as she felt. Behind those glasses she couldn't see his eyes, and that was just as well—she knew how deadly a smile from them could be, she hoped he would keep his sunglasses on all day.

'My car's parked outside,' he said as they left the hotel. As they drove away Quincy caught sight of Penny wandering along with her crammed beach bag over her arm, her face pink from the sun and her bare legs sandy. Penny briefly saw her, and turned her head to stare. Quincy hoped she would see nothing of Joe but black hair blowing in the wind and a pair of sunglasses.

'Did you find your friend?' Joe asked, turning to look at Quincy.

She nodded. 'I hope your parents don't mind having a stranger dumped on them for lunch.'

'You won't be a stranger,' Joe said enigmatically, and before she could ask him what that was supposed to mean he asked: 'How long are you here? When do you go home?'

'We only got here two days ago,' Quincy told him. 'But we're just having a week's holiday, we go home in four days' time.'

'Only a week?' Joe said, his tone flat.

'It was all we could afford,' Quincy muttered. 'We don't have a pop star's income.' No sooner had she said it than she wished she hadn't; it sounded like an accusation, and Joe's brows met.

'I realise that,' he said unsmilingly. 'I was hoping you would be here for longer than that, that's all.'

Quincy felt herself going pink and looked away. For a long time neither of them said anything and the miles zipped by as the sports car weaved and raced along the coast road, leaving every other vehicle behind.

The hotel was large and modern, but was set in beautifully landscaped gardens, lawns sweeping away on every side of the building with trees placed here and there to give a grateful shade, and beds of flowers making splashes of colour in the prevailing green. A swimming pool gleamed very blue beside a raised pink terrace built of some local stone. The terrace was clearly in use as a dining-room; carefully distanced tables under fluttering beach umbrellas, white damask cloths, wine glasses sparkling in the sunlight. People were already eating lunch, waiters moving around between the tables, and from the bar which opened out on to the terrace drifted the sound of a piano.

Quincy followed Joe towards one of the tables, her high heels clicking on the stone floor, looking rather nervously at the two people seated under a blue-striped umbrella.

'Mom, Dad, this is Quincy,' said Joe as they stopped

at the table, and his voice had a faint roughness, almost a trace of uncertainty, she felt, although why he should be worried about introducing her to his parents she couldn't imagine, he must often bring strangers to meet them. Perhaps they did not like meeting strangers? That thought did not make her feel any easier, but she managed to smile as Mr Aldonez rose to offer her his hand. He was more or less the same height as his son, his hair thickly grey, his face thin and weathered, the colour of old leather. His eyes were brown and very shrewd, but they smiled at her as she said shyly: 'Hallo, Mr Aldonez,' and as she smiled back she knew what Joe would look like in thirty years' time.

She was even more nervous about meeting Joe's mother. Everything he had said about her had made it clear how much he loved her, and it mattered so much to Quincy that Mrs Aldonez should like her that as she held out her hand towards the other woman, her palm was damp with perspiration.

'Hallo, Quincy,' Mrs Aldonez said in a slightly accented American voice, the slow lazy warmth of the sun in it, a warmth echoed in her face. Her skin was a warm, sallowed gold; her hair black and sleek, wound in a heavy plait across the top of her head and delicately silvered here and there, her eyes exactly the same colour as Joe's, although the little rays of gold around the pupil were brighter in her case, and her lids were heavier, giving her face a charming placidity which made Quincy feel suddenly less nervous. 'Sit down, what would you like to drink before we order?' Mrs Aldonez asked, and Joe pulled out a chair and stood behind Quincy as she sat down. Briefly she felt his fingertips on her shoulders, the touch something between reassurance and a fleeting caress.

The waiter arrived and cocked an attentive head as Joe repeated: 'Would you like an aperitif?'

Quincy's mind was a blank, she couldn't think, and Joe smiled, glancing at the waiter and ordering for both of them.

'Have you been to Spain before, Quincy?' Mrs Aldonez asked. Her accent, Quincy realised now, was a mixture of American and Spanish.

'No, this is my first visit.'

'Are you enjoying it?'

'Very much, I only wish we weren't going home so soon. I'd like to see more of Spain, it's a fascinating country.'

'You should go into the mountains,' Mrs Aldonez told her. 'You won't get a true impression of Spain from a holiday resort.'

'Perhaps we can take a coach trip one day while we're here,' Quincy agreed.

'Or maybe you can come again soon,' Mrs Aldonez said lazily. 'Spain is a lovely place for a honeymoon.' She slid a smiling look at her husband and then at Joe. 'Isn't it?' she murmured with a distinctly teasing intonation, and both men laughed, although, to Quincy's surprise, Joe flushed slightly. He glanced at her at that second and Quincy felt her heart constrict inside her ribs, making her breathless. She looked away, swallowing. Why had he looked at her like that?

Their drinks arrived and while they sipped them they studied the menu and talked quietly. Quincy said as little as possible, listening intently, however, and absorbing the obvious closeness of the family relationship. Joe's father talked about the weather back home, about his worries for the harvest, his fears mocked cheerfully by Joe, who brushed them aside.

'Every year you say the same,' said Joe, grinning. 'It's always going to be the worst harvest ever. Don't be such a pessimist!'

'It's a professional hazard,' Mrs Aldonez said. 'Farmers are naturally pessimistic, they can't help it.'

'There's nothing natural about it,' said Mr Aldonez. 'We get that way through experience—if there's bad weather around, we always get it right when we're ready to crop.'

'Quincy's not interested in our oranges,' Joe told him, and they all looked at her, smiling.

She flushed. 'I am,' she defended. 'I'm fascinated, until now it never occurred to me that someone grew oranges—they just appeared in the shops and I bought them, I didn't wonder where they came from.'

'Where's your sense of curiosity?' Joe mocked.

'Now that I know something about orange-growing, I'll eat them with far more pleasure,' she promised, and Mrs Aldonez smiled at her.

'Joe plans to give up singing one day and concentrate on the orange groves,' she said. 'He's building himself a new house on some land we just acquired.'

Mr Aldonez nodded approvingly. 'Going to be a fine house,' he said, and Joe asked:

'Are we ready to order yet? The waiters are getting impatient.'

The meal proceeded at a leisurely pace, none of them seemed to be in a hurry and they were the only people on the terrace towards the end of their meal. Quincy sipped her coffee, conscious of a sense of lazy well-being after that superb meal, listening to the talk and looking out over the sunlit gardens. The pool was full of people now, the blue water broken into glittering silver fragments as tanned bodies cut through it. Under a cypress tree the black shadow moved slightly and a girl in a sundress shifted to stay in it, stretching back with a sleepy movement. The air was heavy and somnolent and Quincy felt happy, she did not want to move, to break up the occasion, she wanted to remember this afternoon for ever. She had seen Joe on stage, a public figure; she had seen him tired and drained after a performance. Now she was seeing a very different man and she understood far more about him from the way he talked to his parents—relaxed, casual, lively, laughing as he listened to them. His career rarely got mentioned, they talked about friends or his sister's new baby, about American politics and his father's rheumatism—gradually Quincy realised that Joe's relationship with his family, his involvement with their lives, was the central fact of his world, far more important to him than his career.

When they left the table the afternoon was half gone, the whirr of cicadas deepening around the hotel and a heavy pall of summer heat smothering the air. They walked under the trees in the sleepy shade. Joe talked to his father, leaving Quincy to stroll along beside Mrs Aldonez, who asked her about her own family, her job, her village.

'I've never been to England—I must go one day, your countryside sounds very beautiful.'

'It is, just as lovely as Spain in its way, but far less dramatic. Does Spain seem much changed to you after your years in America?'

She got a wry look. 'That's an understatement, believe me! Changed for the better, too—I haven't seen any of the grinding poverty you once saw here and people aren't in despair, the way they were in the years just before the war.'

'Joe told me how hard your life was,' Quincy told her and Mrs Aldonez smiled.

'He talked to us about you, too.'

Quincy's skin flushed slowly. 'Did he?' What had he said? she wondered.

They were walking so slowly that the two men had drawn far ahead, out of earshot. Mrs Aldonez watched Quincy thoughtfully.

'Does that worry you?'

'That depends what he said, I suppose.' Quincy tried to smile, but didn't do a very good job of it.

'You'd have to ask him,' Mrs Aldonez said with amusement in her face. 'You're not as pretty as I'd expected,' she added, smiling.

'Oh,' said Quincy, not sure how to take that. 'Sorry to disappoint you.' The slight sting in her tone was involuntary and made the other woman laugh.

'I'm not disappointed; on the contrary, I'm delighted.'

Quincy gave her a puzzled look. 'Are you?' What on earth was she talking about? Why should she be delighted to find that Quincy wasn't a raving beauty?

'From what Joe said about you I was expecting more of a glamour girl and he meets so many of those, they throw themselves at him all the time.'

'I'm sure they do,' Quincy agreed, jealousy prickling inside her, and was given another smile.

'Groupies, he calls them—they hang around everywhere he goes, hoping he'll notice them. It worries me at times—Joe's got his head screwed on, he wouldn't be stupid enough to get seriously involved with a girl of that sort, but he's just a man, after all, and men are fools about a pretty woman.'

'You thought I might turn out to be like that? A

groupie?' Quincy said, understanding.

'It seemed likely—Joe said you weren't, of course, but then . . .'

'He's a man and could be wrong?' prompted Quincy in a dry little voice.

His mother gave her an amused look. 'Exactly. That's why I was so delighted when you arrived and I could see you were a nice girl, not especially pretty or glamorous—just ordinary.'

Quincy smiled very brightly with her teeth together. 'Thank you,' she said in a thin little voice, and Mrs Aldonez watched her with increasing amusement.

'Don't look so insulted, I meant it as a compliment. If you'd been beautiful, I'd have been worried, the way Joe has been talking about you. But after seeing you, I know I don't have to worry at all.'

'Well, that's nice to know,' said Quincy, wondering how soon she could safely ask Joe to take her back to her hotel.

Joe and his father had turned back and joined them a moment later. Joe looked at his watch and said: 'I'd better drive Quincy back now, she doesn't want to leave her friend alone for too long.'

Quincy shook hands with his parents, thanked them for the lovely lunch and was surprised to get a kiss from his mother. After what Mrs Aldonez had just said to her, she decided it was some sort of consolation prize for being so dull and ordinary, or possibly a reward for not turning out to be a threat to Mrs Aldonez's peace of mind. A girl as unexciting as Quincy was unlikely to steal Joe, perhaps, and Mrs Aldonez could relax and enjoy her holiday again.

Driving back along the coast, Joe asked: 'Did you really enjoy yourself?'

'Very much,' she said—apart from having her ego
battered to teeny fragments by his mother's remarks,
that was.

'Did you like them?' His tone was eager and Quincy
smiled with involuntary sadness. Joe loved his parents,
he wanted everyone to appreciate them.

'They're both charming, I had a wonderful time, the
lunch was an occasion to remember.' Afterward
hadn't been so terrific, but Mrs Aldonez had not
sounded nasty or unkind, she had merely been speaking her mind frankly and Quincy could understand
why she was worried about the women Joe met on
tour—Quincy worried about that, too.

'I knew you and my mother would hit it off,' he
said, apparently congratulating himself on what he
imagined to be a magic rapport. 'I saw how easily you
were talking to each other after lunch—what was my
mother saying to you?' There was a slight flush in his
face as he asked that and Quincy frowned.

'Oh, nothing special,' she hedged.

'My mother's famous for saying what she thinks,'
said Joe, and there was a definite trace of uneasiness in
his voice.

'I think you could say she did that,' Quincy agreed.

Joe pulled off the road into a layby near some shady
trees. The traffic went snarling past them and the sun
glittered on grey rocks rising at the edge of the swirling
blue sea. Staring straight ahead, Joe tapped his finger
on the wheel in a long silence. Quincy looked at him
uncertainly. Why had he stopped?

'Did she jump the gun, Quincy?' he asked at last,
his voice rough and very low, only just audible.

She wasn't sure what he was talking about and
frowned. Joe turned and looked at her, his mouth un-

steady. 'I didn't think to warn her not to say anything
yet, I thought they realised how things stood.'

'They may—I don't,' said Quincy. 'What are you
talking about, Joe?'

'Us,' he said. 'You, how I feel about you.'

'How do you feel?' she asked huskily, too surprised
to think and feeling her heart turning over inside her
like a porpoise in a sunlit sea, the surprise of sudden,
unexpected joy bursting on her mind and body and
causing dangerous sensations in both.

'Don't you *know*?' he muttered as though she must
know, she had to understand, and, not understanding,
torn by painful winds of confusion and uncertainty and
hope, she looked at him with wide, vulnerable green
eyes, no longer trying to hide her own feelings, aban-
doning any pretence of being indifferent or calm.

Joe moved abruptly and Quincy moved at the same
instant. Their bodies touched, clung; their mouths
meeting in a long kiss. Her eyes closed helplessly, her
arms went round his neck, the heat between them a
growing physical power which made her shudder with
a passion the meeting of their mouths could not
assuage.

When he lifted his head she couldn't meet his eyes,
her face so hot she felt she had sunstroke.

'I've missed you,' he said deeply. 'A hundred times
I planned to fly to England to see you, but I told myself
it was madness. You hate the way I live, I could see
that in London. I couldn't ask you to live the way I
do, you couldn't take it. I told myself to forget you,
but I couldn't. I couldn't get you out of my mind. I
thought about it until I nearly went crazy. I was im-
possible to work with—Billy got close to beating my
brains out! My temper was hair-trigger, I wasn't

sleeping, I couldn't concentrate on my work.' He groaned, and Quincy watched him, a smile in her eyes.

'Poor Joe,' she said, and he gave her a wry look.

'It wasn't funny. Even my family noticed in the end—my mother got it out of me, she always does. She's very persistent, my mother. She uses the water dropping on a stone technique; nag, nag, nag, until she finds out what she wants to know—and then she gives you the benefit of her opinion loud and clear.' He laughed and Quincy half smiled, thinking back over the conversation she had had with Mrs Aldonez—what had Joe's mother really been saying to her? Had she misunderstood all that?

'What did she say to you?' she asked Joe, and he bent and caressed the side of her neck with his fingertips, sending a little shiver of pleasure down her spine. 'She gave me very practical advice—build a house of my own, wind down my career and spend more time at home from now on,' he said huskily.

Quincy looked up at him, doubt in her eyes.

'I can't offer you much,' said Joe, his voice roughening again. 'I've got plenty of money, of course, but at the moment my life is still a crazy mess, I can't offer you much peace. I haven't really got much at all, unless I've got you—and that makes me a taker, rather than a giver. I need you a hell of a lot more than you need me—I realise that. In fact, that's about all I can offer you—the fact that I need you so much it hurts.'

Quincy laughed, close to tears of happiness. 'You're crazy,' she said, and saw him wince.

'I guess I am,' he said. 'I shouldn't have asked, I've no right to try to drag you into the organised insanity that goes on around me most of the time.'

'If that's where you are, that's where I want to be,'

Quincy said, and he looked down at her searchingly, his expression changing. 'I love you, you idiot,' she told him. 'Can't you see that?'

Joe's brown skin took on a deep flush. He caught one of her hands and lifted it to his lips, bending his head over it in a way that pierced Quincy with an almost unbearable happiness. For a few minutes they were alone, their own emotions surrounding them with a crystal wall of silence that excluded the rest of the world. Joe lived in full view of the world, a spotlight always on him. She had felt protective and angry at that concert in London, seeing his isolation in the dangerous glare of those massed eyes, the hunger of the audience reaching out to devour him and absorb the fierce energy he gave off. Joe needed a refuge, a safe place where he could be himself without pretence, without a mask. He would always be under attack, he needed a love which was real, which was human, which was for him as a man, rather than for that glittering icon which the public pursued with such ruthless determination.

A few minutes later, Joe said huskily as he lifted his head again, 'Ever since we've been over in Europe, my mother's been nagging me to go and find you and ask you to marry me—she was getting irritated with me for dragging my feet. She kept asking me how I could know what you would say until I'd taken the risk of asking you, but I was too scared you'd say no, I didn't dare put it to the test.'

Quincy was thinking, her brow furrowed. 'How did you describe me to her?' she asked slowly—what impression had he given his mother, for heaven's sake?

'I told her you were the loveliest girl I'd ever seen,' Joe said. 'I said you'd take her breath away.'

Quincy laughed, relaxing. 'I don't think I did that, not that I noticed, she seemed to have plenty of breath left.' Mrs Aldonez had been welcoming her to the family, she realised, not telling her bluntly that she was no threat to Joe. Looking into Joe's dark eyes with a passion which made them glow with response, she smiled at him. 'If I hadn't come to Spain, then, we might never have met again.' It was a chilling thought.

'We would,' Joe said. 'Sooner or later I'd have plucked up my courage and come to find you—I'd have had to, I need you.' He leaned forward again and kissed her softly, and a car driving past hooted rudely, making Quincy jump. 'Take no notice, my darling,' Joe murmured. 'He's jealous, that's all.' He drew her close again, brushing his lips over her mouth. 'What were we saying?'

'Nothing,' she said, surprised. 'We weren't talking.'

'Good,' said Joe. 'A much overrated pastime, talking. I know a much better one.' And proceeded to demonstrate.

Harlequin Plus

A WORD ABOUT THE AUTHOR

Charlotte Lamb was born and raised in London's East End. To this day she remains at heart an unswerving Londoner, although for the past several years she has lived on the rain-swept Isle of Man in the Irish Sea. Charlotte likens the Isle of Man to the setting of Emily Brontë's *Wuthering Heights* and says that all one can see for miles around are "sheep and heather-covered moors."

Charlotte began writing romances in 1970. Her very first attempt was accepted by Mills & Boon, and she has never looked back.

Since those earlier days, she has become amazingly prolific. Always a fast typist, she can now create and commit to paper at least one novel a month! "I love to write, and it comes easily to me," she explains. "My books practically write themselves."

The fact that Charlotte has been married now for more than two decades, and is the devoted mother of five children ranging in age from seven to twenty, immediately brings to mind the question: where does she find the time to accomplish all her excellent writing? "I have a very good housekeeper," she says with a smile ... as if that explains everything!

Legacy of PASSION

BY CATHERINE KAY

A love story begun long ago comes full circle….

Venice, 1819: Contessa Allegra di Rienzi, young, innocent, unhappily married. She gave her love to Lord Byron—scandalous, irresistible English poet. Their brief, tempestuous affair left her with a shattered heart, a few poignant mementos—and a daughter he never knew about.

Boston, today: Allegra Brent, modern, independent, restless. She learned the secret of her great-great-great-grandmother and journeyed to Venice to find the di Rienzi heirs. There she met the handsome, cynical, blood-stirring Conte Renaldo di Rienzi, and like her ancestor before her, recklessly, hopelessly lost her heart.